Marjorie's Vacation

Carolyn Wells

TABLE OF CONTENTS

MARJORIE'S VACATION
CHAPTER I
MARJORIE'S HOME

In the Maynards' side yard at Rockwell, a swingful of children was slowly swaying back and forth.

The swing was one of those big double wooden affairs that hold four people, so the Maynards just filled it comfortably.

It was a lovely soft summer day in the very beginning of June; the kind of day that makes anybody feel happy but a little bit subdued. The kind of day when the sky is so blue, and the air so clear, that everything seems dreamy and quiet.

But the Maynard children were little, if any, affected by the atmosphere, and though they did seem a trifle subdued, it was a most unusual state of things, and was brought about by reasons far more definite than sky or atmosphere.

Kingdon Maynard, the oldest of the four, and the only boy, was fourteen. These facts had long ago fixed his position as autocrat, dictator, and final court of appeal. Whatever King said, was law to the three girls, but as the boy was really a mild-mannered tyrant, no trouble ensued. Of late, though, he had begun to show a slight inclination to go off on expeditions with other boys, in which girls were not included. But this was accepted by his sisters as a natural course of events, for of course, if King did it, it must be all right.

Next to Kingdon in the swing sat the baby, Rosamond, who was five years old, and who was always called Rosy Posy. She held in her arms a good-sized white Teddy Bear, who was adorned with a large blue bow and whose name was Boffin. He was the child's inseparable companion, and, as he was greatly beloved by the other children, he was generally regarded as a member of the family.

On the opposite seat of the swing sat Kitty, who was nine years old, and who closely embraced her favorite doll, Arabella.

And by Kitty's side sat Marjorie, who was almost twelve, and who also held a pet, which, in her case, was a gray Persian kitten. This kitten was of a most amiable disposition, and was named Puff, because of its fluffy silver fur and fat little body.

Wherever Marjorie went, Puff was usually with her, and oftenest hung over her arm, looking more like a fur boa than a cat.

At the moment, however, Puff was curled up in Marjorie's lap, and was merely a nondescript ball of fur.

These, then, were the Maynards, and though their parents would have said they had four children, yet the children themselves always said, "We are seven," and insisted on considering the kitten, the doll, and the bear as members of the Maynard family.

Kingdon scorned pets, which the girls considered quite the right thing for a boy to do; and, anyway, Kingdon had enough to attend to, to keep the swing going.

"I 'most wish it wasn't my turn," said Marjorie, with a little sigh.
"Of course I want to go for lots of reasons, but I'd love to be in
Rockwell this summer, too."
"As you're not twins you can't very well be in two places at once," said her brother; "but you'll have a gay old time, Mops; there's the new boathouse, you know, since you were there."

"I haven't been there for three years," said Marjorie, "and I suppose there'll be lots of changes."

"I was there two years ago," said Kitty, "but Arabella has never been."

"I'se never been, eever," said Rosy Posy, wistfully, "and so Boffin hasn't, too. But we don't want to go, us wants to stay home wiv Muvver."

"And I say, Mops, look out for the Baltimore oriole," went on Kingdon. "He had a nest in the big white birch last year, and like as not he'll be there again."

"There was a red-headed woodpecker two years ago," said Kitty; "perhaps he'll be there this summer."

"I hope so," said Marjorie; "I'm going to take my big Bird book, and then I can tell them all."

It was the custom in the Maynard household for one of the children to go each summer to Grandma Sherwood's farm near Morristown. They took turns, but as Rosy Posy was so little she had not begun yet.

The children always enjoyed the vacation at Grandma's, but they were a chummy little crowd and dreaded the separation. This was the reason of their subdued and depressed air to-day.

It was Marjorie's turn, and she was to leave home the next morning. Mrs. Maynard was to accompany her on the journey, and then return, leaving Marjorie in the country for three months.

"I wonder how Puffy will like it," she said, as she picked up the kitten, and looked into its blue eyes.

"She'll be all right," said Kingdon, "if she doesn't fight with Grandma's cats. There were about a dozen there last year, and they may object to Puff's style of hair-dressing. Perhaps we'd better cut her hair before she starts."

"No, indeed!" cried Marjorie, "not a hair shall be touched, unless you'd like a lock to keep to remember her while she's gone."

"No, thank you," said King, loftily; "I don't carry bits of cat around in my pockets."

"I'd like a lock," said Kitty; "I'd tie it with a little blue ribbon, and keep it for a forget-me-not. And I'll give you a little curl of Arabella's, and you can keep that to remember her by."

"All right," said Marjorie; "and I'll take a lock of Boffin Bear's hair too. Then I'll have a memento of all the family, because I have pictures of all of you, you know."

With the Maynards to suggest was to act. So the four scrambled out of the swing, and ran to the house.

The Maynard house was a large square affair, with verandas all around. Not pretentious, but homelike and comfortable, and largely given over to the children's use. Though not often in the drawing-room, the four young Maynards frequently monopolized the large living-room, and were allowed free access to the library as well.

Also they had a general playroom and a nursery; and Kingdon had a small den or workroom for his own use, which was oftener than not invaded by the girls.

To the playroom they went, and Kingdon carefully cut small locks from the kitten, the doll, and the bear, and Marjorie neatly tied them with narrow blue ribbons. These mementoes the girls put away, and carefully treasured all through the summer.

Another Maynard custom was a farewell feast at dinner, the night before vacation began. Ordinarily, only the two older children dined with their parents, the other two having their tea in the nursery. But on this occasion, all were allowed at dinner, and the feast was made a special honor for the one who was going away. Gifts were made, as on a birthday, and festival dress was in order.

A little later, then, the four children presented themselves in the library, where their parents awaited them.

Mr. Maynard was a man of merry disposition and rollicking nature, and sometimes joined so heartily in the children's play that he seemed scarcely older than they.

Mrs. Maynard was more sedate, and was a loving mother, though not at all a fussy one. She was glad in many ways to have one of her children spend the summer each year with her mother, but it always saddened her when the time of departure came.

She put her arm around Marjorie, without a word, as the girl came into the room, for it had been three years since the two had been parted, and Mrs. Maynard felt a little sad at the thought of separation.

"Don't look like that, Mother," said Marjorie, "for if you do, I'll begin to feel weepy, and I won't go at all."

"Oh, yes, you will, Miss Midge," cried her father; "you'll go, and you'll stay all summer, and you'll have a perfectly beautiful time. And, then, the first of September I'll come flying up there to get you, and bring you home, and it'll be all over. Now, such a short vacation as that isn't worth worrying about, is it?"

"No," put in Kingdon, "and last year when I went there wasn't any sad good-by."

"That's because you're a boy," said his mother, smiling at him proudly; "tearful good-bys are only for girls and women."

"Yes," said Mr. Maynard, "they enjoy them, you know. Now, I think it is an occasion of rejoicing that Marjorie is to go to Grandma's and have a happy, jolly vacation. We can all write letters to her, and she will write a big budget of a family letter that we can all enjoy together."

"And Mopsy must wite me a little letter, all for my own sef," remarked
Rosy Posy, "'cause I like to get letters all to me."
Baby Rosamond was dressed up for the occasion in a very frilly white frock, and being much impressed by the grandeur of staying up to dinner, she had solemnly seated herself in state on a big sofa, holding Boffin Bear in her arms. Her words, therefore, seemed to have more weight than when she was her everyday roly-poly self, tumbling about on the floor, and Marjorie at once promised that she should have some letters all to herself.

When dinner was announced, Mr. Maynard, with Marjorie, led the procession to the diningroom. They were followed by Mrs. Maynard and Rosamond, and after them came Kingdon and Kitty.

Kitty was a golden-haired little girl, quite in contrast to Marjorie, who had tangled masses of dark, curly hair and large, dark eyes. Her cheeks were round and rosy, and her little white teeth could almost always be seen, for merry Marjorie was laughing most of the time. To-night she wore one of her prettiest white dresses, and her dark curls were clustered at the top of her head into a big scarlet bow. The excitement of the occasion made her cheeks red and her eyes bright, and Mrs. Maynard looked at her pretty eldest daughter with a pardonable pride.

"Midge," she said, "there are just about a hundred things I ought to tell you before you go to Grandma's, but if I were to tell you now, you wouldn't remember one of them; so I have written them all down, and you must take the list with you, and read it every morning so that you may remember and obey the instructions."

Midge was one of the numerous nicknames by which Marjorie was called. Her tumbling, curly hair, which was everlastingly escaping from its ribbon, had gained for her the title of Mops or Mopsy. Midge and Midget had clung to her from babyhood, because she was an active and energetic child, and so quick of motion that she seemed to dart like a midge from place to place. She never did anything slowly. Whether it was an errand for her mother or a game of play, Midge always moved rapidly. Her tasks were always done in half the time it took the other children to do theirs; but in consequence of this haste, they were not always done as well or as thoroughly as could be desired.

This, her mother often told her, was her besetting sin, and Marjorie truly tried to correct it when she thought of it; but often she was too busy with the occupation in hand to remember the good instructions she had received.

4

"I'm glad you did that, Mother," she replied to her mother's remark, "for I really haven't time to study the list now. But I'll promise to read it over every morning at Grandma's, and honest and true, I'll try to be good."

"Of course you will," said her father, heartily; "you'll be the best little girl in the world, except the two you leave here behind you."

"Me's the bestest," calmly remarked Rosamond, who seemed especially satisfied with herself that evening.

"You are," agreed King; "you look good enough to eat, to-night."

Rosamond beamed happily, for she was not unused to flattering observations from the family. And, indeed, she was a delicious-looking morsel of humanity, as she sat in her high chair, and tried her best to "behave like a lady."

The table was decorated with June roses and daisies. The dinner included Marjorie's favorite dishes, and the dessert was strawberries and ice cream, which, Kitty declared, always made a party, anyway.

So with the general air of celebration, and Mr. Maynard's gay chatter and jokes, the little trace of sadness that threatened to appear was kept out of sight, and all through the summer Marjorie had only pleasant memories of her last evening at home.

After the dessert the waitress appeared again with a trayful of parcels, done up in the most fascinating way, in tissue paper and dainty ribbons.

This, too, was always a part of the farewell feast, and Marjorie gave a little sigh of satisfaction, as the well-filled tray was placed before her.

"That's mine! Open mine first!" cried Rosamond, as Marjorie picked up a good-sized bundle.

"Yes, that's Rosy Posy's," said her mother, laughing, "and she picked it out herself, because she thought it would please you. Open it first, Midge."

So Marjorie opened the package, and discovered a little clock, on the top of which was perched a brilliant red bird.

Rosamond clapped her hands in glee. "I knew you'd love it," she cried, "'cause it's a birdie, a yed birdie. And I finded it all mysef in the man's shop. Do you yike it, Mopsy?"

"Indeed I do," cried Marjorie; "it's just what I wanted. I shall keep it on my dressing-table at Grandma's, and then I'll know just when to get up every morning."

"Open mine next," said Kitty; "it's the square flat one, with the blue ribbon."

5

So Marjorie opened Kitty's present and it was a picture, beautifully framed to hang on the wall at Grandma's. The picture was of birds, two beautiful orioles on a branch. The colors were so bright, and so true to nature, that Marjorie exclaimed in delight:

"Now I shall have orioles there, anyway, whether there are real ones in the trees or not. It is lovely, Kitsie, and I don't see how you ever found such a beautiful bird picture."

Marjorie had always been fond of birds, and lately had begun studying them in earnest. Orioles were among her favorites, and so Kitty's picture was a truly welcome gift. King's present came next, and was a beautiful gold pen with a pearl holder.

"That," he explained, "is so you'll write to us often. For I know, Mops, your old penholder is broken, and it's silver, anyway. This is nicer, because it's no trouble to keep it clean and bright."

"That's so, King, and I'm delighted with this one. I shall write you a letter with it, first of all, and I'll tell you all about the farm."

Mrs. Maynard's gift was in a very small parcel, and when Marjorie opened it she found a dear little pearl ring.

"Oh, goody!" she cried. "I do love rings, and I never had one before!
May I wear it always, Mother?"
"Yes," said Mrs. Maynard, smiling. "I don't approve of much jewelry for a little girl not yet twelve years old, but you may wear that."

Marjorie put it on her finger with great satisfaction, and Kitty looked at it lovingly.

"May I have one when I am twelve, Mother?" she asked.

"May I, may I?" chimed in Rosy Posy.

"Yes," said Mr. Maynard; "you girls may each have one just like Marjorie's when you are as old as she is now. That last parcel, Mops, is my present for you. I'm not sure that you can learn to use it, but perhaps you can, and if not I'll take it back and exchange it for something else."

Marjorie eagerly untied the wrappings of her father's gift, and found a little snapshot camera.

"Indeed I can learn to use it," she cried; "I took some pictures once with a camera that belonged to one of the girls at school, and they were all right. Thank you heaps and heaps, father dear; I'll send you pictures of everything on the place; from Grandma herself down to the littlest, weeniest, yellow chicken."

"Next year it will be my turn to go," said Kitty; "I hope I'll get as lovely presents as Mopsy has."

"You will," said Kingdon; "because last year mine were just as good, and so, of course, yours will be."

"I'm sure they will," said Kitty.

CHAPTER II
THE TRIP TO HASLEMERE
The next morning all was bustle and excitement.

Mr. Maynard stayed at home from business to escort the travellers to the train. The trunks were packed, and everything was in readiness for their departure. Marjorie herself, in a spick-and-span pink gingham dress, a tan-colored travelling cloak, and a broad-brimmed white straw hat, stood in the hall saying good-bye to the other children. She carried Puff in her arm, and the sleepy, indifferent kitten cared little whither she was going.

"Be sure," Kingdon was saying, "to plant the seeds I gave you in a sunny place, for if you don't they won't grow right."

"What are the seeds?" asked Marjorie.

"Never mind that," said her brother; "you just plant them in a warm, sunny bed, in good, rich soil, and then you wait and see what comes up. It's a surprise."

"All right, I'll do that, and I suppose Grandma will give me a lot of seeds besides; we always have gardens, you know."

"Be sure to write to me," said Kitty, "about Molly Moss. She's the one that lives in the next house but one to Grandma's. You've never seen her, but I saw her two years ago, and she's an awfully nice girl. You'll like her, I know."

"And what shall I remember to do for you, Rosy Posy?" asked Marjorie, as she kissed the baby good-bye.

"Don't know," responded the little one; "I've never been to Gamma's. Is they piggy-wigs there?"

"No," said Marjorie, laughing; "no piggy-wigs, but some nice ducks."

"All wite; b'ing me a duck."

"I will, if Grandma will give me one"; and then Marjorie was hurried down the steps by her father, and into the carriage, and away she went, with many a backward look at the three children who stood on the veranda waving good-byes to her.

The railroad trip to Morristown lasted about four hours, and Marjorie greatly enjoyed it. Mr. Maynard had put the two travellers into their chairs in the parlor car, and arranged their belongings for them. Marjorie had brought a book to read and a game to play, but with the novel attractions of the trip and the care of her kitten, she was not likely to have time hang heavily on her hands.

Mrs. Maynard read a magazine for a time, and then they were summoned to luncheon in the diningcar. Marjorie thought this great fun, for what is nicer than to be a hungry little girl of twelve, and to eat all sorts of good things, while flying swiftly along in a railroad train, and gazing out of the window at towns and cities rushing by?

Marjorie sat opposite her mother, and observed with great interest the other passengers about. Across the car was a little girl who seemed to be about her own age, and Marjorie greatly wished that they might become acquainted. Mrs. Maynard said that after luncheon she might go and speak to the little stranger if she chose, and Marjorie gladly did so.

"I wonder if you belong in my car," said Marjorie, by way of opening the conversation.

"I don't know," said the other child; "our seats are in the car just back of this."

"We are two cars back," said Marjorie, "but perhaps your mother will let you come into my car a while. I have my kitten with me."

"Where is it?" asked the other little girl.

"I had to leave it with the porter while we came to luncheon. Oh, she's the loveliest kitten you ever saw, and her name is Puff. What's your name?"

"My name is Stella Martin. What's yours?"

"My real name is Marjorie Maynard. But I'm almost always called Midge or Mops or some name like that. We all have nicknames at home; don't you?"

"No, because you see I haven't any brothers or sisters. Mother always calls me Stella."

"Well, let's go and ask her if you can't come into my car for a while.
My mother will look after you, and then you can see the kitten."
After some courteous words of explanation between the two mothers,
Stella was allowed to play with Marjorie for the rest of the journey.
Seated together in one of the big Pullman easy chairs, with the kitten cuddled between them, they rapidly made each other's acquaintance, and soon became good friends. They were not at all alike, for Stella Martin was a thin, pale child with a long braid of straight, light hair, and light blue eyes. She was timid, too, and absolutely devoid of Marjorie's impetuosity and daring. But they were both pleased at the discovery that they were to be near neighbors throughout the summer. Stella's home was next-door to Grandma Sherwood's, although, as both country places were so large, the houses were some distance apart.

Next beyond Stella's house, Marjorie remembered, was where Molly Moss lived, and so the outlook seemed to promise plenty of pleasant company.

About three o'clock in the afternoon the train reached Morristown, and springing out on the platform, Marjorie soon spied Grandma Sherwood's carriage there to meet them. Old Moses was still in charge of the horses, as he had been ever since Marjorie could remember, and in a moment she heard a hearty voice cry, "Oh, there you are!" and there was Uncle Steve waiting for them on the platform.

Uncle Steve was a great friend of Marjorie's, and she flew to greet him almost before he had time to welcome her mother. Then in a few moments the luggage was looked after, and they were all in the carriage, rolling away toward Haslemere.

Marjorie chatted away like a magpie, for she had many questions to ask Uncle Steve, and as she was looking out to renew acquaintance with old landmarks along the road, the drive to the house seemed very short, and soon they were turning in at the gate.

Haslemere was not a large, old-fashioned farm, but a fair-sized and well-kept country place. Grandma Sherwood, who had been a widow for many years, lived there with her son Stephen. It was like a farm, because there were chickens and ducks, and cows and horses, and also a large garden where fresh vegetables of all sorts were raised. But there were no grain fields or large pasture lands, or pigs or turkeys, such as belong to larger farms. The drive from the gate up to the house was a long avenue, shaded on both sides by beautiful old trees, and the wide expanse of lawn was kept as carefully mowed as if at a town house. There were flower beds in abundance, and among the trees and shrubbery were rustic seats and arbors, hammocks and swings, and a delightful tent where the children loved to play. Back of the house the land sloped down to the river, which was quite large enough for delightful boating and fishing.

The house was of that old-fashioned type which has two front doors and two halls, with large parlors between them, and wings on either side. A broad veranda ran across the front, and, turning both corners, ran along either side.

As they drove up to the house, Grandma Sherwood was on the piazza waiting for them. She was not a very old lady, that is, she was not of the white-haired, white-capped, and silver-spectacled variety. She was perhaps sixty years old, and seemed quite as energetic and enthusiastic as her daughter, if perhaps not quite so much so as her granddaughter.

Marjorie sprang out of the carriage, and flew like a young whirlwind to her grandmother's arms, which were open to receive her.

"My dear child, how you have grown!"

"I knew you'd say that, Grandma," said Marjorie, laughing merrily, "and, indeed, I have grown since I was here last. Just think, that was three years ago! I'm almost twelve years old now."

"Well, you are a great girl; run in the house, and lay off your things, while I speak to your mother."

Marjorie danced into the house, flung her coat and gloves on the hall rack, and still holding her kitten, went on through to the kitchen, in search of Eliza the cook.

9

"The saints presarve us!" cried Eliza. "An' is it yersilf, Miss Midget!
Why, yc're as big as a tellygraft pole, so ye are!"
"I know I am, Eliza, but you're just the same as ever; and just look at the kitten I have brought!
Have you any here now?"

"Cats, is it? Indade we have, then! I'm thinkin' there do be a hundred dozen of thim; they're
undher me feet continual! But what kind of a baste is thot ye have there? I niver saw such a
woolly one!"

"This is a Persian kitten, Eliza, and her name is Puff. Isn't she pretty?"

"I'll not be sayin' she's purty, till I see how she doos be behavin'.
Is she a good little cat, Miss Midget dear?"
"Good! Indeed she is a good kitty. And I wish you'd give her some milk,
Eliza, while I run out to see the chickens. Is Carter out there?"
But without waiting for an answer, Marjorie was already flying down through the garden, and
soon found Carter, the gardener, at his work.

"Hello, Carter!" she cried. "How are you this summer?"

"Welcome, Miss Midge! I'm glad to see you back," exclaimed the old gardener, who was very
fond of the Maynard children.

"And I'm glad to be here, Carter; and I have some seeds to plant; will you help me plant
them?"

"That I will. What are they?"

"I don't know; King gave them to me, but he wouldn't tell me what they were."

"Ah, the mischievous boy! Now, how can we tell where to plant them when we don't know
if they'll come up lilies of the valley or elephant's ears?"

Marjorie laughed gayly. "It doesn't matter, Carter," she said; "let's stick them in some sunny
place, and then, if they seem to be growing too high, we can transplant them."

"It's a wise little head you have, Miss; we'll do just that."

Humoring Marjorie's impatience, the good-natured gardener helped her plant the seeds in a
sunny flowerbed, and raked the dirt neatly over them with an experienced touch.

"That looks lovely," said Marjorie, with a satisfied nod of approval; "now let's go and see the
chickens."

This proved even more interesting than she had anticipated, for since her last visit an
incubator had been purchased, and there were hundreds of little chickens of various sizes, in
different compartments, to be looked at and admired.

"Aren't they darlings!" exclaimed Marjorie, as she watched the little yellow balls trying to balance themselves on slender little brown stems that hardly seemed as if they could be meant for legs. "Oh, Carter, I shall spend hours out here every day!"

"Do, Miss Midge; I'll be glad to have you, and the chickens won't mind it a bit."

"Now the horses," Marjorie went on, and off they went to the stables, where Moses had already unharnessed the carriage team, and put them in their stalls. Uncle Steve had a new saddle horse, which came in for a large share of admiration, and the old horse, Betsy, which Grandma Sherwood liked to drive herself, was also to be greeted.

Marjorie loved all animals, but after cats, horses were her favorites.

"Are there any ducks this year, Carter?" she inquired.

"Yes, Miss Midge, there is a duck-pond full of them; and you haven't seen the new boathouse that was built last year for Master Kingdon."

"No, but I want to see it; and oh, Carter, don't you think you could teach me to row?"

"I'm sure of it, Miss Midge; but I hear your grandmother calling you, and I think you'd better leave the boathouse to see to-morrow."

"All right; I think so too, Carter." And Marjorie ran back to the house, her broad-brimmed hat in one hand and her hair ribbon in the other, while her curls were, indeed, in a tangled mop.

CHAPTER III
ON THE ROOF

"Why, Mopsy Maynard," exclaimed her mother, as Marjorie danced into the house, smiling and dishevelled, "what a looking head! Please go straight to your room, and make yourself tidy before supper time."

"Yes, indeed, Mother, but just listen a minute! Uncle Steve has a new horse, a black one, and there are a hundred million little chickens, in the queerest kind of a thing, but I can't remember its name,—it's something like elevator."

"Incubator, perhaps," suggested her mother.

"Yes, that's it; and oh, Mother, it's so funny! Do come out and see it, won't you?"

"Not to-night, child; and now run up to your room and tie up your hair."

Marjorie danced upstairs, singing as she went, but when she reached the door of the room she was accustomed to use, she stopped her singing and stood in the doorway, stock-still with sheer bewilderment.

11

For somehow the room had been entirely transformed, and looked like a totally different apartment.

The room was in one of the wings of the house, and was large and square, with windows on two sides. But these had been ordinary windows, and now they were replaced by large, roomy bay windows, with glass doors that reached from floor to ceiling, and opened out on little balconies. In one of these bay windows was a dear little rocking-chair painted white, and a standard work-basket of dainty white and green wicker, completely furnished with sewing materials. In the other bay window was a dear little writing-desk of bird's-eye maple, and a wicker chair in front of it. The desk was open, and Marjorie could see all sorts of pens and pencils and paper in fascinating array.

But these were only a few of the surprises. The whole room had been redecorated, and the walls were papered with a design of yellow daffodils in little bunches tied with pale green ribbon. The woodwork was all painted white, and entirely around the room, at just about the height of Marjorie's chin, ran a broad white shelf. Of course this shelf stopped for the windows and doors, but the room was large, and there was a great deal of space left for the shelf. But it was the things on the shelf that attracted Marjorie's attention. One side of the room was devoted to books, and Marjorie quickly recognized many of her old favorites, and many new ones. On another side of the room the shelf was filled with flowers, some blooming gayly in pots, and some cut blossoms in vases of water. On a third side of the room the shelf held birds, and this sight nearly took Marjorie's breath away. Some were in gilt cages, a canary, a goldfinch, and another bird whose name Marjorie did not know. And some were stuffed birds of brilliant plumage, and mounted in most natural positions on twigs or branches, or perched upon an ivy vine which was trained along the wall. The fourth side was almost empty, and Marjorie knew at once that it was left so in order that she might have a place for such treasured belongings as she had brought with her.

"Well!" she exclaimed, although there was no one there to hear her. "Well, if this isn't the best ever!" She stood in the middle of the room, and turned slowly round and round, taking in by degrees the furnishings and adornment. All of the furniture was new, and the brass bed and dainty dressing-table seemed to Marjorie quite fit for any princess.

"Well!" she exclaimed again, and as she turned around this time she saw the older people watching her from the hall.

"Oh, Grandma Sherwood!" she cried, and running to the old lady, proceeded to hug her in a way that was more affectionate than comfortable.

"Do you like it?" asked Grandma, when she could catch her breath.

"Like it! It's the most beautiful, loveliest, sweetest room in the whole world! I love it! Did you do it all for me, Grandma?"

"Yes, Midget; that is, I fixed up the room, but for the shelf you must thank Uncle Steve. That is his idea entirely, and he superintended its putting up. You're to use it this year, and next year Kitty can have her dolls and toys on it, and then the year after, King can use it for his fishing-tackle and boyish traps. Though I suppose by that time Rosamond will be old enough to take her turn."

"Then I can't come again for four years," exclaimed Marjorie, with an expression of consternation on her face.

"Not unless you come two at a time," said Grandma; "and I doubt if your mother would consent to that."

"No, indeed," said Mrs. Maynard; "it's hard enough to lose one of the flock, without losing two."

"Well, I'll have a good time with it this summer, anyway," said Marjorie; "can't we unpack my trunk now, Mother, so I can put my pearl pen in my desk; and my clock, that Rosy Posy gave me, on the shelf; and hang up my bird picture on the wall?"

"Not just now," said her mother, "for it is nearly supper time, and you must transform yourself from a wild maid of the woods into a decorous little lady."

The transformation was accomplished, and it was not very long before a very neat and tidy Marjorie walked sedately downstairs to the dining-room. Her white dress was immaculate; a big white bow held the dark curls in place, and only the dancing eyes betrayed the fact that it was an effort to behave so demurely.

"Well, Midget," said Uncle Steve, as they were seated at the supper table, "does the old place look the same?"

"No, indeed, Uncle; there are lots of changes, but best of all is my beauty room. I never saw anything so lovely; I just want to stay up there all the time."

"I thought you'd like that shelf. Now you have room for all the thousand and one bits of rubbish that you accumulate through the summer."

"'Tisn't rubbish!" exclaimed Marjorie, indignantly; "it's dear little birds' nests, and queer kinds of rocks, and branches of strange trees and grasses and things."

"Well, I only meant it sounds to me like rubbish," said Uncle Steve, who loved to tease her about her enthusiasms.

But she only smiled good-naturedly, for she well knew that Uncle Steve was the very one who would take her for long walks in the woods, on purpose to gather this very "rubbish."

The next day Marjorie was up bright and early, quite ready for any pleasure that might offer itself.

Her mother went back home that day, and though Marjorie felt a little sad at parting, yet, after all, Grandma Sherwood's house was like a second home, and there was too much novelty and entertainment all about to allow time for feeling sad.

Moreover, Marjorie was of a merry, happy disposition. It was natural to her to make the best of everything, and even had she had reasons for being truly miserable, she would have tried to be happy in spite of them.

So she bade her mother good-by, and sent loving messages to all at home, and promised to write often.

"Remember," said her mother, as a parting injunction, "to read every morning the list I gave you, which includes all my commands for the summer. When I see you again I shall expect you to tell me that you obeyed them all."

"I will try," said Marjorie; "but if it is a long list I may forget some of them sometimes. You know, Mother, I AM forgetful."

"You are, indeed," said Mrs. Maynard, smiling; "but if you'll try I think you'll succeed, at least fairly well. Good-by now, dear; I must be off; and do you go at once to your room and read over the list so as to start the day right."

"I will," said Marjorie, and as soon as she had waved a last good-by, and the carriage had disappeared from view, she ran to her room, and sitting down at her pretty desk, unfolded the list her mother had given her.

To her great surprise, instead of the long list she had expected to find, there were only two items. The first was, "Keep your hands clean, and your hair tidy"; and the other read, "Obey Grandma implicitly."

"Well," thought Marjorie to herself, "I can easily manage those two! And yet," she thought further, with a little sigh, "they're awfully hard ones. My hands just WON'T keep clean, and my hair ribbon is forever coming off! And of course I MEAN to obey Grandma always; but sometimes she's awful strict, and sometimes I forget what she told me."

But with a firm resolve in her heart to do her best, Marjorie went downstairs, and went out to play in the garden.

Some time later she saw a girl of about her own age coming down the path toward her. She was a strange-looking child, with a very white face, snapping black eyes, and straight wiry black hair, braided in two little braids, which stood out straight from her head.

"Are you Marjorie?" she said, in a thin, piping voice. "I'm Molly Moss, and I've come to play with you. I used to know Kitty."

"Yes," said Marjorie, pleasantly, "I'm Marjorie, and I'm Kitty's sister. I'm glad you came. Is that your kitten?"

"Yes," said Molly, as she held up a very small black kitten, which was indeed an insignificant specimen compared to the Persian beauty hanging over Marjorie's arm.

"It's a dear kitten," Molly went on. "Her name is Blackberry. Don't you like her?"

"Yes," said Marjorie, a little doubtfully; "perhaps she can be company for Puff. This is my Puff." Marjorie held up her cat, but the two animals showed very little interest in one another.

"Let's put them to sleep somewhere," said Molly, "and then go and play in the loft."

The kittens were soon deposited in the warm kitchen, and the two girls ran back to the barn for a good play. Marjorie had already begun to like Molly, though she seemed rather queer at first, but after they had climbed the ladder to the warm sweet-smelling hay-loft, they grew better acquainted, and were soon chattering away like old friends.

Molly was not at all like Stella Martin. Far from being timid, she was recklessly daring, and very ingenious in the devising of mischief.

"I'll tell you what, Mopsy," she said, having already adopted Marjorie's nickname, "let's climb out of the window, that skylight window, I mean, onto the roof of the barn, and slide down. It's a lovely long slide."

"We'll slide off!" exclaimed Marjorie, aghast at this proposition.

"Oh, no, we won't; there's a ledge at the edge of the roof, and your heels catch that, and that stops you. You CAN'T go any further."

"How do you get back?"

"Why, scramble back up the roof, you know. Come on, it's lots of fun."

"I don't believe Grandma would like it," said Marjorie, a little doubtfully.

"Oh, pshaw, you're afraid; there's no danger. Come on and try it, anyhow."

Now Marjorie did not like to be called afraid, for she really had very little fear in her disposition. So she said: "Well, I'll go up the ladder and look out, and if it looks dangerous I won't do it."

"Not a bit of danger," declared Molly. "I'll go up first." Agile as a sprite, Molly quickly skipped up the ladder, and opened the trap-door in the barn roof. Sticking her head up through, she soon drew her thin little body up after it and called to Marjorie to follow. Marjorie was a much heavier child, but she sturdily climbed the ladder, and then with some difficulty clambered out on the roof.

"Isn't it gay?" cried Molly, and exhilarated by the lofty height, the novel position, and the excitement of the moment, Marjorie thought it was.

"Now," went on Molly, by way of instruction, "sit down beside me right here at the top. Hang on with your hands until I count three and then let go, and we'll slide straight down the roof."

Marjorie obeyed directions, and sat waiting with a delightful feeling of expectancy.

"One, two, three!" counted Molly, and at the last word the two girls let go their grasp and slid.

Swiftly and lightly the slender little Molly slid to the gutter of the eaves of the roof, caught by her heels, and stopped suddenly, leaning against the slanted roof, comfortably at her ease.

Not so Marjorie. She came swiftly down, and, all unaccustomed to motion of this sort, her feet struck the gutter, her solid little body bounced up into the air, and instead of falling backward again, she gave a frightened convulsive movement, and fell headlong to the ground.

Quick as a flash, Molly, when she saw what had happened, scrambled back up the roof with a wonderful agility, and let herself down through the skylight, and down the ladder like lightning. She rushed out of the barn, to where Marjorie lay, and reached her before Carter did, though he came running at the first sounds of Marjorie's screams.

"I'm not hurt much," said Marjorie, trying to be brave; "if you'll help me, Carter, I think I can walk to the house."

"Walk nothin'," growled Carter; "it's Miss Mischief you are for sure! I thought you had outgrown your wild ways, but you're just as bad as ever! What'll your grandma say?"

Molly stood by, decidedly scared. She didn't know how badly Marjorie was hurt, and she longed to comfort her, and tell her how sorry she was that she had urged her to this mischief, but Carter gave her no opportunity to speak. Indeed, it was all she could do to keep up with the gardener's long strides, as he carried Marjorie to the house. But Molly was no coward, and she bravely determined to go to the house with them, and confess to Mrs. Sherwood that she was to blame for the accident.

But when they reached the door, and Grandma Sherwood came out to meet them, she was so anxious and worried about Marjorie that she paid little attention to Molly's efforts at explanation.

"What are you trying to say, child?" she asked hastily of Molly, who was stammering out an incoherent speech. "Well, never mind; whatever you have to say, I don't want to hear it now. You run right straight home; and if you want to come over to-morrow to see how Marjorie is, you may, but I can't have you bothering around here now. So run home."

And Molly ran home.

CHAPTER IV
A PAPER-DOLL HOUSE
The result of Marjorie's fall from the roof was a sprained ankle. It wasn't a bad sprain, but the doctor said she must stay in bed for several days.

"But I don't mind very much," said Marjorie, who persisted in looking on the bright side of everything, "for it will give me a chance to enjoy this beautiful room better. But, Grandma, I can't quite make out whether I was disobedient or not. You never told me not to slide down the roof, did you?"

"No, Marjorie; but your common-sense ought to have told you that. I should have forbidden it if I had thought there was the slightest danger of your doing such a thing. You really ought to have known better."

Grandma's tone was severe, for though she was sorry for the child she felt that Marjorie had done wrong, and ought to be reproved.

Marjorie's brow wrinkled in her efforts to think out the matter.

"Grandma," she said, "then must I obey every rule that you would make if you thought of it, and how shall I know what they are?"

Grandma smiled. "As I tell you Midget, you must use your common-sense and reason in such matters. If you make mistakes the experience will help you to learn; but I am sure a child twelve years old ought to know better than to slide down a steep barn roof. But I suppose Molly put you up to it, and so it wasn't your fault exactly."

"Molly did suggest it, Grandma, but that doesn't make her the one to blame, for I didn't have to do as she said, did I?"

"No, Midge; and Molly has behaved very nicely about it. She came over here, and confessed that she had been the ringleader in the mischief, and said she was sorry for it. So you were both to blame, but I think it has taught you a lesson, and I don't believe you'll ever cut up that particular trick again. But you certainly needn't be punished for it, for I think the consequences of having to stay in bed for nearly a week will be punishment enough. So now we're through with that part of the subject, and I'm going to do all I can to make your imprisonment as easy for you as possible."

It was in the early morning that this conversation had taken place, and Grandma had brought a basin of fresh, cool water and bathed the little girl's face and hands, and had brushed out her curls and tied them up with a pretty pink bow.

Then Jane came with a dainty tray, containing just the things Marjorie liked best for breakfast, and adorned with a spray of fresh roses. Grandma drew a table to the bedside and piled pillows behind Marjorie's back until she was quite comfortable.

"I feel like a queen, Grandma," she said; "if this is what you call punishment I don't mind it a bit."

"That's all very well for one day, but wait until you have been here four or five days. You'll get tired of playing queen by that time."

"Well, it's fun now, anyway," said Marjorie, as she ate strawberries and cream with great relish.

After breakfast Jane tidied up the room, and Marjorie, arrayed in a little pink kimono, prepared to spend the day in bed. Grandma brought her books to read and writing materials to write letters home, and Marjorie assured her that she could occupy herself pleasantly.

So Grandma went away and left her alone. The first thing Marjorie did was to write a letter to her mother, telling her all about the accident. She had thought she would write a letter to each of the children at home, but she discovered to her surprise that it wasn't very easy to write sitting up in bed. Her arms became cramped, and as she could not move her injured ankle her whole body grew stiff and uncomfortable. So she decided to read. After she had read what seemed a long time, she found that that, too, was difficult under the circumstances. With a little sigh she turned herself as well as she could and looked at the clock. To her amazement, only an hour had elapsed since Grandma left her, and for the first time the little girl realized what it meant to be deprived of the free use of her limbs.

"Only ten o'clock," she thought to herself; "and dinner isn't until one!"

Not that Marjorie was hungry, but like all the invalids she looked forward to meal-times as a pleasant diversion.

But about this time Grandma reappeared to say that Molly had come over to see her.

Marjorie was delighted, and welcomed Molly gladly.

"I'm awful sorry," the little visitor began, "that I made you slide down the roof."

"You didn't make me do it," said Marjorie, "it was my fault quite as much as yours; and, anyway, it isn't a very bad sprain. I'll be out again in a few days, and then we can play some more. But we'll keep down on the ground,—we can't fall off of that."

"I thought you might like to play some games this morning," Molly suggested, "so I brought over my jackstraws and my Parcheesi board."

"Splendid!" cried Marjorie, delighted to have new entertainment.

In a few moments Molly had whisked things about, and arranged the jackstraws on a small table near the bed. But Marjorie could not reach them very well, so Molly changed her plan.

"I'll fix it," she said, and laying the Parcheesi board on the bed, she climbed up herself, and sitting cross-legged like a little Turk, she tossed the jackstraws out on the flat board, and the game began in earnest.

They had a jolly time and followed the jackstraws with a game of
Parcheesi.
Then Jane came up with some freshly baked cookies and two glasses of milk.

"Why, how the time has flown!" cried Marjorie, "it's half-past eleven, and it doesn't seem as if you'd been here more than five minutes, Molly."

18

"I didn't think it was so late, either," and then the two girls did full justice to the little luncheon, while the all-useful Parcheesi board served as a table.

"Now," said Marjorie, when the last crumbs had disappeared, "let's mix up the two games. The jackstraws will be people, and your family can live in that corner of the Parcheesi board, and mine will live in this. The other two corners will be strangers' houses, and the red counters can live in one and the blue counters in the other. This place in the middle will be a park, and these dice can be deer in the park."

"Oh, what fun!" cried Molly, who was not as ingenious as Marjorie at making up games, but who was appreciative enough to enter into the spirit of it at once.

They became so absorbed in this new sort of play that again the time flew and it was dinner-time before they knew it.

Grandma did not invite Molly to stay to dinner, for she thought Marjorie ought to rest, but she asked the little neighbor to come again the next morning and continue their game.

After dinner Grandma darkened the room and left Marjorie to rest by herself, and the result of this was a long and refreshing nap.

When she awoke, Grandma appeared again with fresh water and towels, and her afternoon toilet was made. Marjorie laughed to think that dressing for afternoon meant only putting on a different kimono, for dresses were not to be thought of with a sprained ankle.

And then Uncle Steve came in.

Uncle Steve was always like a ray of sunshine, but he seemed especially bright and cheery just now.

"Well, Midget Mops," he said, "you have cut up a pretty trick, haven't you? Here, just as I wanted to take you driving, and walking in the woods, and boating, and fishing, and perhaps ballooning, and airshipping, and maybe skating, here you go and get yourself laid up so you can't do anything but eat and sleep! You're a nice Midget, you are! What's the use of having an Uncle Steve if you can't play with him?"

"Just you wait," cried Marjorie; "I'm not going to be in bed more than a few days, and I'm going to stay here all summer. There'll be plenty of time for your fishing and skating yet."

"But unless I get you pretty soon, I'll pine away with grief. And everybody out on the farm is lonesome for you. The horses, Ned and Dick, had made up their minds to take you on long drives along the mountain roads where the wild flowers bloom. They can't understand why you don't come out, and they stand in their stalls weeping, with great tears rolling down their cheeks."

Marjorie laughed gayly at Uncle Steve's foolery, and said: "If they're weeping so you'd better take them some of my pocket handkerchiefs."

"Too small," said Uncle Steve, scornfully; "one of your little handkerchiefs would get lost in Dick's eye or Ned's ear. And old Betsy is weeping for you too. Really, you'll have to get around soon, or those three horses will run away, I fear."

"What about the cow; does she miss me?" asked Marjorie, gravely, though her eyes were twinkling.

"The cow!" exclaimed Uncle Steve. "She stands by the fence with her head on the top rail, and moos so loud that I should think you could hear her yourself. She calls 'Mopsy, Mopsy, Moo,' from morning till night. And the chickens! Well, the incubator is full of desolate chickens. They won't eat their meal, and they just peep mournfully, and stretch their little wings trying to fly to you."

"And the dogs?" prompted Marjorie.

"Oh, the dogs—they howl and yowl and growl all the time. I think I'll have to bring the whole crowd of animals up here. They're so anxious to see you."

"Do, Uncle Steve. I'd be glad to see them, and I'm sure they'd behave nicely."

"I think so. The cow could sit in that little rocking-chair, and the three horses could sit on the couch, side by side. And then we could all have afternoon tea."

Marjorie shook with laughter at the thought of the cow sitting up and drinking afternoon tea, until Uncle Steve declared that if she laughed so hard she'd sprain her other ankle. So he said he would read to her, and selecting a book of fairy tales, he read aloud all the rest of the afternoon. It was delightful to hear Uncle Steve read, for he would stop now and then to discuss the story, or he would put in some funny little jokes of his own, and he made it all so amusing and entertaining that the afternoon flew by as if on wings.

Then Jane came again with the pretty tray of supper, and after that Grandma and Marjorie had a nice little twilight talk, and then the little girl was tucked up for the night, and soon fell asleep.

When she woke the next morning and lay quietly in bed thinking over of the events of the day before, she came to the conclusion that everybody had been very kind to her, but that she couldn't expect so much attention every day. So she made up her mind that when she had to spend hours alone, she would try to be good and patient and not trouble Grandma more than she could help.

Then she thought of the written list her mother had given her. She smiled to think how easy it was now to keep those commands. "Of course," she thought, "I can keep my hands clean and my hair tidy here, for Grandma looks after that herself; and, of course, I can't help obeying her while I'm here, for she doesn't command me to do anything, and I couldn't do it if she did."

Molly came again that morning, and as Grandma had asked her to stay to dinner with Marjorie, the girls prepared for a good morning's play.

It was astonishing how many lovely things there were to play, even when one of the players couldn't move about.

Molly had brought over her paper-doll's house, and as it was quite different from anything Marjorie had ever seen before, she wondered if she couldn't make one for herself, and so double the fun of the game.

Grandma was consulted, but it was Uncle Steve who brought them the necessary materials to carry out their plan.

A paper-doll's house is quite different from the other kind of a doll's house, and Molly's was made of a large blankbook.

So Uncle Steve brought a blankbook almost exactly like it for Marjorie, and then he brought her scissors, and paste, and several catalogues which had come from the great shops in the city. He brought, too, a pile of magazines and papers, which were crammed full of illustrated advertisements.

The two little girls set busily to work, and soon they had cut out a quantity of chairs, tables, beds, and furniture of all sorts from the pictured pages.

These they pasted in the book. Each page was a room, and in the room were arranged appropriate furniture and ornaments.

The parlor had beautiful and elaborate furniture, rugs, pictures, bric-a-brac, and even lace curtains at the windows. The library had beautiful bookcases, writing-desk, reading-table and a lamp, easy-chairs, and everything that belongs in a well-ordered library.

The dining-room was fully furnished, and the kitchen contained everything necessary to the satisfaction of the most exacting cook.

The bedrooms were beautiful with dainty brass beds, chintz-covered furniture, and dressing-tables fitted out with all sorts of toilet equipments.

All of these things were found in the catalogues and the magazine advertisements; and in addition to the rooms mentioned, there were halls, a nursery, playroom, and pleasant verandas fitted up with hammocks and porch furniture.

Of course it required some imagination to think that these rooms were in the shape of a house, and not just leaves of a book, but both Midge and Molly had plenty of imagination, and besides it was very practical fun to cut out the things, and arrange them in their places. Sometimes it was necessary to use a pencil to draw in any necessary article that might be missing; but usually everything desired could be found, from potted palms to a baby carriage.

Marjorie grew absorbed in the work, for she dearly loved to make things, and her ingenuity suggested many improvements on Molly's original house.

21

CHAPTER V

SOME INTERESTING LETTERS

The family for the paper-doll house was selected from the catalogues that illustrate ready-made clothing. Beautiful gentlemen were cut out, dressed in the most approved fashions for men. Charming ladies with trailing skirts and elaborate hats were found in plenty. And children of all ages were so numerous in the prints that it was almost difficult to make a selection. Then, too, extra hats and wraps and parasols were cut out, which could be neatly put away in the cupboards and wardrobes which were in the house. For Marjorie had discovered that by pasting only the edges of the wardrobe and carefully cutting the doors apart, they could be made to open and shut beautifully.

Uncle Steve became very much interested in these wonderful houses, and ransacked his own library for pictures to be cut up.

Indeed, so elaborate did the houses grow to be, Molly's being greatly enlarged and improved, that they could not be finished in one morning.

But Grandma was not willing to let Marjorie work steadily at this occupation all day, and after dinner Molly was sent home, and the paper dolls put away until the next day.

"But I'm not ill, Grandma," said Marjorie; "just having a sprained ankle doesn't make me a really, truly invalid."

"No, but you must rest, or you will get ill. Fever may set in, and if you get over-excited with your play, and have no exercise, you may be in bed longer than you think for. Besides, I think I remember having heard something about implicit obedience, and so I expect it now as well as when you're up on your two feet."

"I don't think I can help obeying," said Marjorie, roguishly, "for I can't very well do anything else. But I suppose you mean obey without fretting; so I will, for you are a dear, good Grandma and awfully kind to me."

With a parting pat on her shoulder, Grandma left the little girl for her afternoon nap, and Marjorie would have been surprised at herself had she known how quickly she fell asleep.

Uncle Steve made it a habit to entertain her during the later hours of each afternoon, and, although they were already great chums, his gayety and kindness made Marjorie more than ever devoted to her uncle.

This afternoon he came in with a handful of letters.

"These are all for you," he said; "it is astonishing what a large correspondence you have."

Marjorie was amazed. She took the budget of letters her uncle handed her and counted five. They were all duly stamped, and all were postmarked, but the postmarks all read Haslemere.

"How funny!" exclaimed Marjorie; "I didn't know there was a post office at Haslemere."

"You didn't!" exclaimed Uncle Steve; "why, there certainly is. Do you mean to say that you don't know that there's a little post office in the lowest branch of that old maple-tree down by the brook?"

"You mean just where the path turns to go to the garden?"

"That's the very spot. Only this morning I was walking by there, and I saw a small post office in the tree. There was a key in the door of it, and being curious, I opened it, and looked in. There I saw five letters for you, and as you're not walking much this summer, I thought I'd bring them to you. I brought the key, too."

As he finished speaking, Uncle Steve drew from his pocket a little bright key hung on a blue ribbon, which he gravely presented to Marjorie. Her eyes danced as she took it, for she now believed there was really a post office there, though it was sometimes difficult to distinguish Uncle Steve's nonsense from the truth.

"Now I'm more than ever anxious to get well," she cried, "and go out to see that post office."

"Oh, no," said Uncle Steve, shaking his head; "you don't care about post offices and walks in the woods, and drives through the country. You'd rather slide down an old barn roof, and then lie in bed for a week."

"Catch me doing it again," said Marjorie, shaking her head decidedly; "and now, Uncle, suppose we open these letters."

"Why, that wouldn't be a bad idea. Here's a paper-cutter. Let's open one at a time, they'll last longer. Suppose you read this one first."

Marjorie opened the first letter, and quickly turned the page to see the signature.

"Why, Uncle Steve," she cried, "this is signed Ned and Dick! I didn't know horses could write letters."

"There are a great many things, my child, that you don't know yet. And so Ned and Dick have written to you! Now that's very kind of them. Read me what they say."

In great glee, Marjorie read aloud:

"DEAR MARJORIE:
It is too bad
For you to act this way;
Just think what fun we might have had
Out driving every day.
"We could have gone to Blossom Banks,
Or Maple Grove instead;
But no, you had to cut up pranks
That landed you in bed!
"We hope you'll soon be well again,

23

And get downstairs right quick;
And we will all go driving then.
Your true friends,
NED AND DICK."

"Well, I do declare," said Uncle Steve, "I always said they were intelligent horses, but this is the first time I've ever heard of their writing a letter. They must be very fond of you, Marjorie."

Marjorie's eyes twinkled. She well knew Uncle Steve had written the letter himself, but she was always ready to carry out her part of a joke, so she replied:

"Yes, I think they must be fond of me, and I think I know somebody else who is, too. But it was nice of Ned and Dick to write and let me know that they hadn't forgotten me. And as soon as I can get downstairs, I shall be delighted to go driving with them. Where is Blossom Banks, Uncle?"

"Oh, it's a lovely place, a sort of picnic ground; there are several grassy banks, and blossoms grow all over them. They slope right down to the river; but, of course, you wouldn't think them nearly so nice as a sloping barn roof."

Marjorie knew she must stand teasing from Uncle Steve, but his smile was so good-natured, and he was such a dear old uncle anyway, that she didn't mind it very much.

"Suppose I read another letter," she said, quite ready to turn the subject.

"Do; open that one with the typewritten address. I wonder who could have written that! Perhaps the cow; she's very agile on the typewriter."

The mental picture of the cow using the typewriter produced such hilarity that it was a few moments before the letter was opened.

"It IS from the cow!" exclaimed Marjorie, "and she does write beautifully on the machine. I don't see a single error."

"Read it out, Midge; I always love to hear letters from cows."

So Marjorie read the cow's note:

"Mopsy Midge, come out to play;
I've waited for you all the day.
In the Garden and by the brook,
All day for you I vainly look.
With anxious brow and gaze intense
I lean against the old rail fence,
And moo and moo, and moo, and moo,
In hopes I may be heard by you.
And if I were not so forlorn,
I think I'd try to blow my horn.

Oh, come back, Midget, come back now,
And cheer your lonely, waiting
Cow."

"Now, that's a first-class letter," declared Uncle Steve. "I always thought that cow was a poet. She looks so romantic when she gazes out over the bars. You ought to be pleased, Marjorie, that you have such loving friends at Haslemere."

"Pleased! I'm tickled to death! I never had letters that I liked so well. And just think, I have three left yet that I haven't opened. I wonder who they can be from."

"When you wonder a thing like that, it always seems to me a good idea to open them and find out."

"I just do believe I will! Why, this one," and Marjorie hastily tore open another letter, "this one, Uncle, is from old Bet!"

"Betsy! That old horse! Well, she must have put on her spectacles to see to write it. But I suppose when she saw Ned and Dick writing, she didn't want them to get ahead of her, so she went to work too. Well, do read it, I'm surely interested to hear old Betsy's letter."

"Listen then," said Marjorie:

"DEAR LITTLE MIDGE:
        I'm lonesome here,
    Without your merry smiles to cheer.
    I mope around the livelong day,
    And scarcely care to munch my hay.
    I am so doleful and so sad,
    I really do feel awful bad!
    Oh hurry, Midge, and come back soon;
    Perhaps to-morrow afternoon.
    And then my woe I will forget,
    And smile again.
Your lonesome BET"

"Well, she is an affectionate old thing," said Uncle Steve; "and truly, Midget, I thought she was feeling lonesome this morning. She didn't seem to care to eat anything, and she never smiled at me at all."

"She's a good old horse, Uncle, but I don't like her as much as I do Ned and Dick. But don't ever tell Betsy this, for I wouldn't hurt her feelings for anything."

"Oh, yes, just because Ned and Dick are spirited, fast horses you like them better than poor, old Betsy, who used to haul you around when you were a baby."

"Oh, I like her well enough; and, anyway, I think a heap more of her now, since she wrote me such an affectionate letter. Now, Uncle, if you'll believe it, this next one is from the

25

chickens! Would you have believed that little bits of yellow chickens, in an incubator, could write a nice, clear letter like this? I do think it's wonderful! Just listen to it:

"DEAR MOPSY:
　Why
　Are you away?
　We weep and cry
　All through the day.
　"Oh, come back quick,
　Dear Mopsy Mop!
　Then each small chick
　Will gayly hop.
　"We'll chirp with glee,
　No more we'll weep;
　Each chickadee
　Will loudly peep."

"Well, that's certainly fine, Midget, for such little chickens. If it were the old hen, now, I wouldn't be so surprised, for I see her scratching on the ground every day. I suppose she's practising her writing lesson, but I never yet have been able to read the queer marks she makes. But these little yellow chickadees write plainly enough, and I do think they are wonderfully clever."

"Yes, and isn't it funny that they can rhyme so well, too?"

"It is, indeed. I always said those Plymouth Rocks were the smartest chickens of all, but I never suspected they could write poetry."

"And now, Uncle, I've only one left." Marjorie looked regretfully at the last letter, wishing there were a dozen more. "But I can keep them and read them over and over again, I like them so much. I'd answer them, but I don't believe those animals read as well as they write."

"No," said Uncle Steve, wagging his head sagely, "I don't believe they do. Well, read your last one, Mops, and let's see who wrote it."

"Why, Uncle, it's from the dogs! It's signed 'Nero and Tray and Rover'! Weren't they just darling to write to me! I believe I miss the dogs more than anything else, because I can have Puffy up here with me."

Marjorie paused long enough to cuddle the little heap of grey fur that lay on the counterpane beside her, and then proceeded to read the letter:

　"Dear Mopsy Midget,
　We're in a fidget,
　Because we cannot find you;
　We want to know
　How you could go
　And leave your dogs behind you!
　"We bark and howl,

And snarl and yowl,
And growl the whole day long;
You are not here,
And, Mopsy dear,
We fear there's something wrong!
"We haven't heard;
Oh, send us word
Whatever is the matter!
Oh, hurry up
And cheer each pup
With laughter and gay chatter."

"That's a very nice letter," said Marjorie, as she folded it up and returned it to its envelope. "And I do think the animals at Haslemere are the most intelligent I have ever known. Uncle, I'm going to send these letters all down home for King and Kitty to read, and then they can send them back to me, for I'm going to keep them all my life."

"I'll tell you a better plan than that, Midget. If you want the children to read them, I'll make copies of them for you to send home. And then I'll tell you what you might do, if you like. When I go downtown I'll buy you a great big scrapbook, and then you can paste these letters in, and as the summer goes on, you can paste in all sorts of things; pressed leaves or flowers, pictures and letters, and souvenirs of all sorts. Won't that be nice?"

"Uncle Steve, it will be perfectly lovely! You do have the splendidest ideas! Will you get the book to-morrow?"

"Yes, Miss Impatience, I will."

And that night, Marjorie fell asleep while thinking of all the lovely things she could collect to put in the book, which Uncle Steve had told her she must call her Memory Book.

CHAPTER VI
BOO!

The days of Marjorie's imprisonment went by pleasantly enough. Every morning Molly would come over, and they played with their paper-doll houses. These houses continually grew in size and beauty. Each girl added a second book, which represented grounds and gardens. There were fountains, and flowerbeds and trees and shrubs, which they cut from florists' catalogues; other pages were barns and stables, and chicken-coops, all filled with most beautiful specimens of the animals that belonged in them. There were vegetable gardens and grape arbors and greenhouses, for Uncle Steve had become so interested in this game that he brought the children wonderful additions to their collections.

It was quite as much fun to arrange the houses and grounds as it was to play with them, and each new idea was hailed with shrieks of delight.

Molly often grew so excited that she upset the paste-pot, and her scraps and cuttings flew far and wide, but good-natured Jane was always ready to clear up after the children. Jane had been with Mrs. Sherwood for many years, and Marjorie was her favorite of all the grandchildren, and she was never too tired to wait upon her. She, too, hunted up old books and papers that might contain some contributions to the paper-doll houses. But afternoons were always devoted to rest, until four or five o'clock, when Uncle Steve came to pay his daily visit.

One afternoon he came in with a fresh budget of letters.

"Letters!" exclaimed Marjorie. "Goody! I haven't had any letters for two days. Please give them to me, Uncle, and please give me a paper-cutter."

"Midge," said Uncle Steve, "if you think these are letters, you're very much mistaken. They're not."

"What are they, then?" asked Marjorie, greatly mystified, for they certainly looked like letters, and were sealed and stamped.

"As I've often told you, it's a good plan to open them and see."

Laughing in anticipation at what she knew must be some new joke of Uncle Steve's, Marjorie cut the envelopes open. The first contained, instead of a sheet of paper, a small slip, on which was written:

"If you think this a letter, you're much mistook; It's only a promise of a New Book!"

"Well," said Marjorie, "that's just as good as a letter, for if you promise me a book, I know I'll get it. Oh, Uncle, you are such a duck! Now I'll read the next one."

The next one was a similar slip, and said:

"This isn't a letter, though like one it seems; It's only a promise of Chocolate Creams!"
"Oh!" cried Marjorie, ecstatically, "this is just too much fun for anything! Do you mean real chocolate creams, Uncle?"

"Oh, these are only promises. Very likely they don't mean anything."

"YOUR promises do; you've never broken one yet. Now I'll read another:

"This isn't a letter, dear Marjorie Mops, It's only a promise of Peppermint Drops!"
"Every one is nicer than the last! And now for the very last one of all!"

Marjorie cut open the fourth envelope, and read:

"Dear Mopsy Midget, this isn't a letter; It's only a promise of something much better!"

"Why, it doesn't say what!" exclaimed Midge, but even as she spoke, Jane came into the room bringing a tray.

She set it on the table at Marjorie's bedside, and Marjorie gave a scream of delight when she saw a cut-glass bowl heaped high with pink ice cream.

"Oh, Uncle Steve!" she cried, "the ice cream is the 'something better,'
I know it is, and those other parcels are the other three promises! Can
I open them now?"
Almost without waiting for her question to be answered, Marjorie tore off papers and strings, and found, as she fully expected, a box of chocolate creams, a box of peppermint drops, and a lovely new story book.

Then Grandma came in to their tea party and they all ate the ice cream, and Marjorie declared it was the loveliest afternoon tea she had ever attended.

Even Puff was allowed to have a small saucer of the ice cream, for she was a very dainty kitten, and her table manners were quite those of polite society.

But the next afternoon Uncle Steve was obliged to go to town, and Marjorie felt quite disconsolate at the loss of the jolly afternoon hour.

But kind-hearted Grandma planned a pleasure for her, and told her she would invite both Stella Martin and Molly to come to tea with Marjorie from four till five.

Marjorie had not seen Stella since the day they came up together on the train, and the little girls were glad to meet again. Stella and Molly were about as different as two children could be, for while Molly was headstrong, energetic, and mischievous, Stella was timid, quiet, and demure.

Both Marjorie and Molly were very quick in their actions, but Stella was naturally slow and deliberate. When they played games, Stella took as long to make her move as Molly and Midge together. This made them a little impatient, but Stella only opened her big blue eyes in wonder and said, "I can't do things any faster." So they soon tired of playing games, and showed Stella their paper-dolls' houses. Here they were the surprised ones, for Stella was an adept at paper dolls and knew how to draw and cut out lovely dolls, and told Marjorie that if she had a paintbox she could paint them.

"I wish you would come over some other day, Stella, and do it," said Midge; "for I know Uncle Steve will get me a paint-box if I ask him to, and a lot of brushes, and then we can all paint. Oh, we'll have lots of fun, won't we?"

"Yes, thank you," said Stella, sedately.

Marjorie giggled outright. "It seems so funny," she said, by way of explanation, "to have you say 'yes, thank you' to us children; I only say it to grown people; don't you, Molly?"

"I don't say it at all," confessed Molly; "I mean to, but I 'most always forget. It's awful hard for me to remember manners. But it seems to come natural to Stella."

Stella looked at her, but said nothing. She was a very quiet child, and somehow she exasperated Marjorie. Perhaps she would not have done so had they all been out of doors, playing together, but she sat on a chair by Marjorie's bedside with her hands folded in her lap, and her whole attitude so prim that Marjorie couldn't help thinking to herself that she'd like to stick a pin in her. Of course she wouldn't have done it, really, but Marjorie had a riotous vein of mischief in her, and had little use for excessive quietness of demeanor, except when the company of grown-ups demanded it.

But Stella seemed not at all conscious that her conduct was different from the others, and she smiled mildly at their rollicking fun, and agreed quietly to their eager enthusiasms.

At last Jane came in with the tea-tray, and the sight of the crackers and milk, the strawberries and little cakes, created a pleasant diversion.

Stella sat still in her chair, while Marjorie braced herself up on her pillows, and Molly, who was sitting on the bed, bounced up and down with glee.

Marjorie was getting much better now, so that she could sit upright and preside over the feast. She served the strawberries for her guests, and poured milk for them from the glass pitcher.

Molly and Marjorie enjoyed the good things, as they always enjoyed everything, but Stella seemed indifferent even to the delights of strawberries and cream.

She sat holding a plate in one hand, and a glass of milk in the other, and showed about as much animation as a marble statue. Even her glance was roving out of the window, and somehow the whole effect of the child was too much for Marjorie's spirit of mischief.

Suddenly, and in a loud voice, she said to Stella, "BOO!"

This, in itself, was not frightful, but coming so unexpectedly it startled Stella, and she involuntarily jumped, and her glass and plate fell to the floor with a crash; and strawberries, cakes, and milk fell in a scattered and somewhat unpleasant disarray.

Marjorie was horrified at what she had done, but Stella's face, as she viewed the catastrophe, was so comical that Marjorie went off into peals of laughter. Molly joined in this, and the two girls laughed until the bed shook.

Frightened and nervous at the whole affair, Stella began to cry. And curiously enough, Stella's method of weeping was as noisy as her usual manner was quiet. She cried with such loud, heart-rending sobs that the other girls were frightened into quietness again, until they caught sight of Stella's open mouth and tightly-closed but streaming eyes, when hilarity overtook them again.

Into this distracting scene, came Grandma. She stood looking in amazement at the three children and the debris on the floor.

At first Mrs. Sherwood naturally thought it an accident due to Stella's carelessness, but Marjorie instantly confessed.

"It's my fault, Grandma," she said; "I scared Stella, and she couldn't help dropping her things."

"You are a naughty girl, Mischief," said Grandma, as she tried to comfort the weeping Stella. "I thought you would at least be polite to your little guests, or I shouldn't have given you this tea party."

"I'm awfully sorry," said Marjorie, contritely; "please forgive me,
Stella, but honestly I didn't think it would scare you so. What would
YOU do, Molly, if I said 'boo' to you?"
"I'd say 'boo yourself!'" returned Molly, promptly.

"I know you would," said Marjorie, "but you see Stella's different, and I ought to have remembered the difference. Don't cry, Stella; truly I'm sorry! Don't cry, and I'll give you my— my paper-doll's house."

This was generous on Marjorie's part, for just then her paper-doll's house was her dearest treasure.

But Stella rose to the occasion.

"I w-wont t-take it," she said, still sobbing, though trying hard to control herself; "it wasn't your fault, Marjorie; I oughtn't to have been so silly as to be scared b-because you said b-boo!"

By this time Jane had removed all evidences of the accident, and except for a few stains on Stella's frock, everything was in order.

But Stella, though she had quite forgiven Marjorie, was upset by the whole affair, and wanted to go home.

So Grandma declared she would take the child home herself and apologize to Mrs. Martin for Marjorie's rudeness.

"It was rude, Marjorie," she said, as she went away; "and I think Molly must go home now, and leave you to do a little thinking about your conduct to your other guest."

So Marjorie was left alone to think, and half an hour later Grandma returned.

"That was a naughty trick, Marjorie, and I think you ought to be punished for it."

"But, Grandma," argued Miss Mischief, "I wasn't disobedient; you never told me not to say boo to anybody."

"But I told you, dear, that you must use your common-sense; and you must have known that to startle Stella by a sudden scream at her was enough to make her drop whatever she was holding."

31

"Grandma, I 'spect I was mischievous; but truly, she did look so stiff and pudgy, I just HAD to make her jump."

"I know what you mean, Midge; and you have a natural love of mischief, but you must try to overcome it. I want you to grow up polite and kind, and remember those two words mean almost exactly the same thing. You knew it wasn't kind to make Stella jump, even if it hadn't caused her to upset things."

"No, I know it wasn't, Grandma, and I'm sorry now. But I'll tell you what: whenever Stella comes over here again, I'll try to be SPECIALLY kind to her, to make up for saying boo!"

CHAPTER VII
A BOAT-RIDE

Great was the rejoicing of the whole household when at last Marjorie was able to come downstairs once more.

Uncle Steve assisted her down. He didn't carry her, for he said she was far too much of a heavyweight for any such performance as that, but he supported her on one side, and with a banister rail on the other she managed beautifully.

And, anyway, her ankle was just about as well as ever. The doctor had not allowed the active child to come downstairs until there was little if any danger that an imprudence on her part might injure her again.

It was Saturday afternoon, and though she could not be allowed to walk about the place until the following week, yet Uncle Steve took her for a long, lovely drive behind Ned and Dick, and then brought her back to another jolly little surprise.

This was found in a certain sheltered corner of one of the long verandas. It was so built that it was almost like a cosy, little square room; and climbing vines formed a pleasant screen from the bright sunlight. To it Uncle Steve had brought a set of wicker furniture: dear little chairs and a table and a settee, all painted green. Then there was a green-and-white hammock swung at just the right height, and containing two or three fat, jolly-looking, green pillows, in the midst of which Puff had chosen to curl herself up for a nap.

There was a little bamboo bookcase, with a few books and papers, and a large box covered with Japanese matting, which had a hinged lid, and was lovely to keep things in. There was a rug on the floor, and Japanese lanterns hung from the ceiling, all in tones of green and white and silver.

Marjorie unceremoniously dislodged Puff from her comfortable position, and flung herself into the hammock instead.

"Uncle Steve!" she exclaimed, grabbing that gentleman tightly round the neck as he leaned over her to adjust her pillows, "you are the best man in the whole world, and I think you ought to be President! If you do any more of these lovely things for me I shall just—just SUFFOCATE with joy. What makes you so good to me, anyhow?"

"Oh, because you're such a little saint, and never do anything naughty or mischievous!"

"That's a splendid reason," cried Marjorie, quite appreciating the joke, "and, truly, Uncle Steve,—don't you tell,—it's a great secret: but I AM going to try to be more dignified and solemn."

This seemed to strike Uncle Steve as being very funny, for he sat down on the little wicker settee and laughed heartily.

"Well, you may as well begin now, then; and put on your most dignified and pompous manner, as you lie there in that hammock, for I'm going to read to you until tea-time."

"Goody, goody!" cried Marjorie, bobbing up her curly head, and moving about excitedly. "Please, Uncle, read from that new book you brought me last night. I'll get it!"

"That's a nice, dignified manner, that is! Your Serene Highness will please calm yourself, and stay just where you are. I shall select the book to read from, and I shall do the reading. All you have to do is to lie still and listen."

So Marjorie obeyed, and, of course, Uncle Steve picked out the very book she wanted, and read to her delightfully for an hour or more.

Marjorie's porch, as it came to be called, proved to be a favorite resort all summer long for the family and for any guests who came to the house. Marjorie herself almost lived in it for the first few days after she came downstairs, but at last the doctor pronounced her ankle entirely well, and said she might "start out to find some fresh mischief."

So the next morning, directly after breakfast, she announced her intention of going down to see the boathouse.

"Just think," she exclaimed, "I have never seen it yet, and King told me to go down there the very first thing."

"I suppose you'll come back half-drowned," said Grandma, "but as you seem unable to learn anything, except by mistakes, go ahead. But, Marjorie, do try not to do some absurd thing, and then say that I haven't forbidden it! I don't forbid you to go in the boat, if Carter goes with you, but I do forbid you to go alone. Will you remember that?"

"Yes, Grandma, truly I will," said Marjorie, with such a seraphic smile that her grandmother kissed her at once.

"Then run along and have a good time; and don't jump off the dock or anything foolish."

"I won't," cried Marjorie, gayly; and then she went dancing down the path to the garden. Carter was in the greenhouse potting some plants.

"Carter," said Marjorie, putting her head in at the door, "are you very busy?"

"Busy, indeed! I have enough work here with these pesky plants to keep me steady at it till summer after next. Busy, is it? I'm so busy that the bees and the ants is idle beside me. Busy? Well, I AM busy!"

But as the good-natured old man watched Marjorie's face, and saw the look of disappointment settling upon it, he said: "But what matters that? If so be, Miss Midget, I can do anything for you, you've only to command."

"Well, Carter, I thought this morning I'd like to go down to see the boathouse; and I thought, perhaps,—maybe, if you weren't busy, you might take me for a little row in the boat. Just a little row, you know—not very far."

It would have taken a harder heart than Carter's to withstand the pleading tones and the expectant little face; and the gardener set down his flower-pots, and laid down his trowel at once.

"Did your grandmother say you could go, Miss Midget?"

"She said I could go if you went with me."

"Then it's with ye I go, and we'll start at once."

Marjorie danced along by the side of the old man as he walked more slowly down the garden path, when suddenly a new idea came into her head.

"Oh, Carter," she cried, "have my seeds come up yet? And what are the flowers? Let's go and look at them."

"Come up yet, is it? No, indeed, they've scarcely settled themselves down in the earth yet."

"I wish they would come up, I want to see what they'll be. Let's go and look at the place where we planted them, Carter."

So they turned aside to the flowerbed where the precious seeds had been planted, but not even Marjorie's sharp eyes could detect the tiniest green sprout. With an impatient little sigh she turned away, and as they continued down toward the boathouse, Marjorie heard somebody calling, and Molly Moss came flying up to her, all out of breath.

"We were so afraid we wouldn't catch you," she exclaimed, "for your Grandma said you had gone out in the boat."
"We haven't yet," answered Marjorie, "but we're just going. Oh, Carter, can we take Molly, too?"

"And Stella," added Molly. "She's coming along behind."

Sure enough, Stella was just appearing round the corner of the house, and walking as sedately as if on her way to church.

"Hurry up, Stella," called Marjorie. "Can we all go, Carter?"

"Yes, if yees'll set still in the boat and if the other little lady gets here before afternoon. She's the nice, quiet child, but you two are a pair of rascally babies, and I don't know whether it's safe to go on the water with ye. I'm thinkin' I'll take little Miss Stella, and leave ye two behind."

"I don't think you will, Carter," said Marjorie, not at all alarmed by the old man's threat. "I think you'll take all three of us, and we'll sit as still as mice, won't we, Molly?"

"Yes," said Molly; "can we take off our shoes and stockings and hang our feet over the sides of the boat?"

"Oh, yes," cried Marjorie, "that will be lots of fun!"

"Indeed you'll do nothing of the sort," and Carter's honest old face showed that he felt great anxiety concerning his madcap charges. "Ye must promise to sit still, and not move hand or foot, or I'll go back to my work and leave yees on shore."

This awful suggestion brought about promises of strictly good behavior, and as Stella had arrived, the party proceeded to the boathouse.

Stella was mildly pleased at the prospect of a row, and walked demurely by Carter's side, while the other two ran on ahead and reached the boathouse first.

As the door was locked, and they could not open it, Marjorie, who was all impatience to see the boat, proposed that they climb in the window. Molly needed no second invitation, and easily slipped through the little square window, and Marjorie, with a trifle more difficulty, wriggled her own plump little body through after.

As the window was not on the side of the boathouse toward which Carter was approaching, he did not see the performance, and so when he and Stella reach the boathouse a few moments later, they could see nothing at all of the other two girls.

"Merciful powers!" he exclaimed. "Whatever has become of them two witches?"

"Where can they be?" cried Stella, clasping her hands, and opening her eyes wide in alarm.

Old Carter was genuinely frightened. "Miss Marjorie!" he called, loudly. "Miss Molly! Where be ye?"

Meanwhile, the two girls inside the boathouse had carefully scrambled down into the boat and sat quietly on the stern seat. There was a strong breeze blowing, and as the boat swayed up and down on the rippling water, its keel grating against the post to which it was tied, and the doors and windows being tightly shut, they did not hear Carter's voice. They really had no intention of frightening the old man, and supposed he would open the door in a moment.

But Carter's mind was so filled with the thought that the children had fallen into the water that it didn't occur to him to open the boathouse. He went to the edge of the pier, which was a narrow affair, consisting only of two wooden planks and a single hand rail, and gazed anxiously down into the water.

This gave Stella a firm conviction that the girls were drowned, and without another word she began to cry in her own noisy and tumultuous fashion. Poor Carter, already at his wits' end, had small patience with any additional worry.

"Keep still, Miss Stella," he commanded; "it's enough to have two children on me hands drowned without another one raising a hullabaloo. And it's a queer thing, too, if them wicked little rats is drownded, why they don't come up to the surface! My stars! Whatever will the Missus say? But, havin' disappeared so mortal quick, there's no place they can be but under the water. I'll get a boat-hook, and perhaps I can save 'em yet."

Trembling with excitement and bewildered with anxiety, so that he scarcely knew what he did, the old man fitted the key in the lock. He flung open the boathouse door and faced the two children, who sat quietly and with smiling faces in the boat.

"Well, if ye don't beat all! Good land, Miss Marjorie, whatever did ye give me such a scare for? Sure I thought ye was drownded, and I was jest goin' to fish ye up with a boat-hook! My, but you two are terrors! And how did ye get in now? Through the keyhole, I suppose."

"Why, no, Carter," exclaimed Marjorie, who was really surprised at the old man's evident excitement; "we were in a hurry, and the door was locked, so we just stepped in through the window."

"Stepped in through the window, is it? And if the window had been locked ye'd have jest stepped in through the chimley! And if the chimley had been locked, ye'd have stepped into the water, and ducked under, and come up through the floor! When ye're in a hurry, ye stop for nothin', Miss Midget."

The old man's relief at finding the children safe was so great that he was really talking a string of nonsense to hide his feelings.

But Stella, though she realized the girls were all right, could not control her own emotions so easily, and was still crying vociferously.

"For goodness' sake!" exclaimed Molly, "what IS the matter with Stella?
Doesn't she want to go boating?"
"Why—yes," sobbed Stella, "b-but I thought you two were drowned."

"Well, we're not!" cried Marjorie, gayly. "So cheer up, Stella, and come along."

Leaving the two girls, as they were already seated, in the stern of the boat, Carter carefully tucked Stella into the bow seat, and then took his own place on the middle thwart. This arrangement enabled him to keep his eye on the two mischievous madcaps, and he had no fear that Stella would cut up any tricks behind his back.

He could not reprove the mischief-makers, for they had done nothing really wrong, but he looked at them grimly as he rowed out into the stream.

"Oh," exclaimed Marjorie, "isn't this just too lovely for anything! Please, Carter, mayn't we just put our hands in the water if we keep our feet in the boat?"

"No," growled Carter; "you'll be wantin' to put your heads in next. Now do set still, like the nice young lady behind me."

Anxious to be good, Marjorie gave a little sigh and folded her hands in her lap, while Molly did likewise.

Carter's eyes twinkled as he looked at the two little martyrs, and his heart relented.

"Ye may just dangle your fingers in the water, if ye want to," he said, "but ye must be careful not to wobble the boat."

The children promised, and then gave themselves up to the delight of holding their hands in the water and feeling the soft ripples run through their fingers.

The row down the river was perfect. The balmy June day, with its clear air and blue sky, the swift, steady motion of the boat impelled by Carter's long, strong strokes, and the soothing sensation of the rushing water subdued even the high spirits of Midge and Molly into a sort of gentle, tranquil happiness.

CHAPTER VIII
A MEMORY BOOK
With a few deft strokes Carter brought the boat to land on a long, smooth, shelving beach. A crunch of the keel on the pebbles, and then the boat was half its length on shore. Stella, in the bow, grasped the sides of the boat tightly with both hands, as if the shore were more dangerous than the water. Carter stepped out, and drew the boat well up on land, and assisted the girls out.

Stella stepped out gingerly, as if afraid of soiling her dainty boots; but Midge and Molly, with a hop, skip, and jump, bounded out on the beach and danced round in glee.

"I do believe," cried Marjorie, "that this is Blossom Banks! For there are three banks, one after another, just covered with wild flowers. And as true as I live there's a scarlet tanager on that bush! Don't startle him, Stella."

Molly laughed at the idea of Stella startling anything, and softly the girls crept nearer to the beautiful red bird, but in a moment he spread his black-tipped wings and flew away.

"It is Blossom Banks, Miss Midge," said Carter, who now came up to the girls, and who was carrying a mysterious-looking basket. He had secured the boat, and seemed about to climb the banks.

"What's in the basket, Carter?" cried Midge. "Is it a picnic? Is it a truly picnic?"

"Well, just a wee bit of a picnic, Miss Midget. Your Grandma said that maybe some cookies and apples wouldn't go begging among yees. But ye must climb the banks first, so up ye go!"

Gayly the girls scrambled up the bank, and though Stella was not as impetuous as the others, she was not far behind. At every step new beauties dawned, and Marjorie, who was a nature-lover, drew a long breath of delight as she reached the top of the Blossom Banks.

They trotted on, sometimes following Carter's long strides and sometimes dancing ahead; now falling back to chatter with Stella and now racing each other to the next hillock.

At last they reached the dearest little picnic place, with soft green grass for a carpet, and gnarled roots of great trees for rustic seats.

"For a little picnic," said Midge, as she sat with an apple in one hand and a cookie in the other, contentedly munching them both alternately, "this is the bestest ever. And isn't this a splendiferous place for a big picnic!"

"Perhaps your grandma will let you have one this summer," said Stella. "She had one for Kingdon last year and we all came to it. It was lovely fun."

"Indeed it was," cried Molly; "there were swings on the trees, and we played tag, and we had bushels of sandwiches."

"I'm going to ask Grandma as soon as ever I get home," declared Midge, "and I 'most know she'll let me have one. But I don't know many children around here to ask."

"I'll make up a list for you," volunteered Molly. "Come on, girls, let's play tag."

The cookies and apples being all gone and Carter having consented in response to their coaxing to stay half an hour longer, they had a glorious game of tag.

Stella, though so sedate when walking, could run like a deer, and easily caught the others; for Marjorie was too plump to run fast, and Molly, though light on her feet, was forever tumbling down.

At last, tired and warm from their racing, they sat down again in the little mossy dell and played jackstones until Carter declared they must go home.

"All right," said Midge; "but, Carter, row us a little farther down stream, won't you, before you turn around?"

"I will, Miss Midge, if ye'll sit still and not be everlastin' makin' me heart jump into me throat thinkin' ye'll turn the boat upside down."

"All right," cried Midge, and she jumped into the boat with a spring and a bounce that made the other end tip up and splash the water all over her.

"There ye go now," grumbled Carter; "my, but it's the rambunctious little piece ye are! Now, Miss Molly, for the land's sake, do step in with your feet and not with your head! You two'll be the death of me yet!"

Carter's bark was worse than his bite, for, although he scolded, he helped the children in carefully and gently seated Stella in her place. Then he stepped in, and with a mighty shove of the oar pushed the boat off the beach, and they were afloat again.

The exhilaration of the occasion had roused Midge and Molly to a high state of frolicsomeness, and it did seem impossible for them to keep still. They dabbled their hands in the water and surreptitiously splashed each other, causing much and tumultuous giggling. This was innocent fun in itself, but Carter well knew that a sudden unintentional bounce on the part of either might send the other one into the water. Regardless of their entreaties he turned around and headed the boat for home.

"Ye're too many for me, Miss Midge," he exclaimed; "if I land you safe this trip ye can get somebody else to row ye the next time. I'm having nervous prostration with your tricks and your didoes. NOW, will ye be good?"

This last exasperated question was caused by the fact that a sudden bounce of Molly's caused the boat to lurch and Carter's swift-moving oar sent a drenching wave all over Midge.

"Pooh, water doesn't hurt!" cried the victim. "I like it. Do it again, Molly!"
"Don't you do it, Miss Molly!" roared Carter, bending to his oars and pulling fast in an effort to get home before these unmanageable children had passed all bounds.

"Girls," piped Stella, plaintively from her end of the boat, "if you don't stop carrying on, I shall cry."

This threat had more effect than Carter's reprimands, and, though the two madcaps giggled softly, they did sit pretty still for the remainder of the trip.

Once more on the dock, Marjorie shook herself like a big dog, and declared she wasn't very wet, after all. "And I'm very much obliged to you, Carter," she said, smiling at the old man; "you were awful good to take us for such a lovely boat-ride, and I'm sorry we carried on so, but truly, Carter, it was such a lovely boat that I just couldn't help it! And you do row splendid!"

The compliment was sincere, and by no means made with the intention of softening Carter's heart, but it had that effect, and he beamed on Midget as he replied:

"Ah, that's all right, me little lady. Ye just naturally can't help bouncin' about like a rubber ball. Ye have to work off yer animal spirits somehow, I s'pose. But if so be that ye could sit a bit quieter, I might be injuced to take ye agin some other day. But I'd rather yer grandma'd be along."

"Oho!" laughed Marjorie. "It would be funny to have Grandma in a boat! She'd sit stiller than Stella, and I don't believe she'd like it, either."

With Stella in the middle, the three girls intertwined their arms and skipped back to the house. Marjorie and Molly had found that the only way to make Stella keep up with them was to urge her along in that fashion.

"Good-by," said Marjorie, as the three parted at the gate; "be sure to come over to-morrow morning; and, Stella, if you'll bring your paintbox, it will be lovely for you to paint those paper dolls."

The three girls had become almost inseparable companions, and though Midge and Molly were more congenial spirits, Stella acted as a balance wheel to keep them from going too far. She really had a good influence over them, though exerted quite unconsciously; and Midge and Molly inspired Stella with a little more self-confidence and helped her to conquer her timidity.

"Good-by," returned Stella, "and be sure to have a letter in the post office by four o'clock, when James goes for the milk."

The post office in the old maple tree had become quite an institution, and the girls put letters there for each other nearly every day, and sent for them by any one who might happen to be going that way.

Quiet little Stella was especially fond of getting letters and would have liked to receive them three times a day.

The elder members of the three families often sent letters or gifts to the children, and it was not at all unusual to find picture postcards or little boxes of candy, which unmistakably came from the generous hand of Uncle Steve.

One delightful afternoon Marjorie sat in her cosy little porch with a table full of delightful paraphernalia and a heart full of expectation.

She was waiting for Uncle Steve, who was going to devote that afternoon to helping her arrange her Memory Book. Marjorie had collected a quantity of souvenirs for the purpose, and Uncle Steve had bought for her an enormous scrapbook. When she had exclaimed at its great size, he had advised her to wait until it had begun to fill up before she criticised it; and when she looked at her pile of treasures already accumulated, she wondered herself how they would all get in the book.

At last Uncle Steve came, and sitting down opposite Marjorie at her little table, announced himself as ready to begin operations.

"We'll plan it out a little first, Mopsy, and then fasten the things in afterward."

Marjorie was quite content to sit and look on, at least until she found out how such things were done.

"You see," said her uncle, "we'll take a page for each occasion—more or less. For instance, as this book is to represent just this summer it ought to begin with your trip up here. Have you anything that reminds you of that day?"

"Yes," said Marjorie, looking over her heap of treasures, "here's a little kind of a badge that father bought for me at the station as we were going to the train."

"Just the thing; now, you see, as this is on a pin itself we'll just stick it in this first page. Anything else?"

"Well, here's a pretty picture I cut out of a magazine on the train coming up; oh, and here are two postcards that I bought of a boy who brought them through the train."

"Fine! Now, you see, we'll paste all these on this page and anything more if you have it, and then every time you look at this page you can just seem to see that whole trip, can't you?"

"Yes," said Marjorie, who was becoming absorbedly interested in this new game; "and here's the time-table, Uncle: but that isn't very pretty and it's so big. Oh, and here's the card, the bill of fare, you know, that we had in the dining-car. See, it has a picture on it."

"Why, Midget, it isn't considered exactly good form to carry the MENU away with you; but it's really no crime, and since you have it, we'll put it in. As to the time-table, we'll just cut out this part that includes the stations at the beginning and end of your trip. See?"

"Oh, yes, indeed I do! And what a beautiful page!" Marjorie breathlessly watched as Uncle Steve arranged the souvenirs harmoniously on the big page and pasted them neatly in their places. Then, taking from his pocket a box of colored pencils, he printed at the top of the page, in ornate letters, the date and the occasion. Uncle Steve was an adept at lettering, and the caption was an additional ornament to the already attractive page.

Thus they went on through the book. Sometimes a page was devoted to a special occasion, and again many scattered mementoes were grouped together. It seemed as if every pleasure Marjorie had had since she came, had produced something attractive for her book.

A fancy lace paper represented the big box of bonbons that her father had sent her when she had her sprained ankle. Many photographs there were, for Marjorie had learned to use her camera pretty well, and Uncle Steve sometimes took snap-shots of the children with his own larger camera. There were several little pictures that Stella had painted for her, an old tintype that Grandma had given her, a feather from the tail of Marjorie's pet rooster, and many such trifles, each of which brought up a host of memories of pleasant or comical situations.

The sprained-ankle episode filled up several pages. For there were the letters that Marjorie had received from the animals, and other notes and pictures that had been sent to her, and many mementoes of those long days she had spent in bed. The beautiful book Uncle Steve had brought her at that time was suggested by its title, cut from the paper wrapper which had been on the book when it came. Indeed, it seemed that there was no end to the ingenious ways of remembering things that Marjorie wanted to remember. A tiny, bright bird feather would recall the walk she took with Grandma one afternoon; a pressed wild flower was an eloquent reminder of Blossom Banks; and a large strawberry hull, neatly pasted into place, Marjorie insisted upon to remind her of the day when she said "Boo" to Stella.

Several pages were devoted to souvenirs from home, and Rosy Posy's illegible scrawls were side by side with neatly-written postcards from her parents.

All of these things Uncle Steve arranged with the utmost care and taste, and Marjorie soon learned how to do it for herself. Some things, such as letters or thin cards, must be pasted in; heavier cards or postcards were best arranged by cutting slits for the corners and tucking them in; while more bulky objects, such as pebbles, a tiny china doll or a wee little Teddy Bear, must be very carefully tied to the page by narrow ribbons put through slits from the back.

Marjorie was so impetuous and hasty in her work that it was difficult for her to learn to do it patiently and carefully. Her first efforts tore the pages and were far from being well done. But, as she saw the contrast between her own untidy work and Uncle Steve's neat and careful effects, she tried very hard to improve, and as the book went on her pages grew every day better and more careful.

At the top of each page Uncle Steve would write the date or the place in dainty, graceful letters; and often he would write a name or a little joke under the separate souvenirs, until, as time went on, the book became one of Marjorie's most valued and valuable possessions.

CHAPTER IX
THE FRONT STAIRS
Marjorie had been at Grandma Sherwood's about weeks, and as a general thing she had been a pretty good little girl. She had tried to obey her mother's orders, and though it was not easy to keep her troublesome curls always just as they ought to be and her ribbon always in place, yet she had accomplished this fairly well, and Grandma said that she really deserved credit for it.

But to obey Grandma implicitly was harder still. Not that Marjorie ever meant to disobey or ever did it wilfully, but she was very apt to forget and, too, it seemed to be natural for her to get into mischief. And as it was always some new sort of mischief, which no one could have thought of forbidding, and as she was always so sorry for it afterward, there was more or less repentance and forgiveness going on all the time.

But, on the whole, she was improving, and Uncle Steve sometimes said that he believed she would live to grow up without tumbling off of something and breaking her neck, after all.

Grandma Sherwood found it far easier to forgive Marjorie's unintentional mischief than her forgetting of explicit commands.

One command in particular had caused trouble all summer. There were two front doors to Grandma's house and two halls. One of these halls opened into the great drawing-room on one side and a smaller reception room on the other, where callers were received. The stairs in this hall were of polished wood and were kept in a state of immaculate, mirror-like shininess by Jane, who took great pride in this especial piece of work.

The other front door opened into a hall less pretentious. This hall was between the drawingroom and the family library, and the stairs here were covered with thick, soft carpet.

It was Grandma's wish that the members of the family should usually use the carpeted stairs, for she too took great pride in the glossy, shining surface of the others. Uncle Steve preferred the carpeted stairs, anyway, as they led to the upper hall which opened into his own room, and Grandma invariably used them.

As a means of distinction, the wooden stairs were habitually called the Front Stairs; and, though they were equally front, the carpeted flight was always spoken of as the Other Stairs.

From the first, Marjorie had been explicitly forbidden to go up and down the Front Stairs; and from the first Marjorie had found this rule most difficult to remember.

Rushing from her play into the house, often with muddy or dusty shoes, she would fly into the hall, clatter up the Front Stairs, and, perhaps, down again and out, without a thought of her wrongdoing. This would leave footprints, and often scratches and heel-marks on the beautiful steps, which meant extra work for Jane; and even then the scratches were not always effaceable.

Many a serious talk had Grandma and Marjorie had on the subject; many times had Marjorie faithfully promised to obey this particular command; and, alas! many times had the child thoughtlessly broken her promise.

At last, Grandma said: "I know, my dear, you do not MEAN to forget, but you DO forget. Now this forgetting must stop. If you run up those Front Stairs again, Marjorie, I'm going to punish you."

"Do, Grandma," said Marjorie, cheerfully; "perhaps that will make me stop it. For honest and true I just resolve I won't do it, and then before I know it I'm just like Jack and the Beanstalk, 'a-hitchet, a-hatchet, a-up I go!' and, though I don't mean to, there I am!"

Grandma felt like smiling at Marjorie's naive confession, but she said very seriously: "That's the trouble, dearie, you DO forget and you must be made to remember. I hope it won't be necessary, but if it is, you'll have to be punished."

"What will the punishment be, Grandma?" asked Marjorie, with great interest. She was hanging around Mrs. Sherwood's neck and patting her face as she talked. There was great affection between these two, and though Marjorie was surprised at the new firmness her grandmother was showing, she felt no resentment, but considerable curiosity.

"Never mind; perhaps you'll never deserve punishment and then you will never know what it would have been. Indeed, I'm not sure myself, but if you don't keep off those Front Stairs we'll both of us find out in short order."

Grandma was smiling, but Marjorie knew from her determined tone that she was very much in earnest.

For several days after that Marjorie kept carefully away from the Front Stairs, except when she was wearing her dainty house slippers. It was an understood exception that, when dressed for dinner or on company occasions and her feet shod with light, thin-soled shoes, Marjorie might walk properly up or down the Front Stairs. The restriction only applied to her heavy-soled play shoes or muddied boots.

So all went well, and the question of punishment being unnecessary, it was almost forgotten.

One morning, Marjorie was getting ready to go rowing with Carter. Molly was to go too, and as the girls had learned to sit moderately still in the boat, the good-natured gardener frequently took them on short excursions.

It was a perfect summer day, and Marjorie sang a gay little tune as she made herself ready for her outing. She tied up her dark curls with a pink ribbon, and as a hat was deemed unnecessary by her elders, she was glad not to be bothered with one. She wore a fresh, pink gingham dress and thick, heavy-soled shoes, lest the boat should be damp. She took with her a small trowel, for she was going to dig some ferns to bring home; and into her pocket she stuffed a little muslin bag, which she always carried, in case she found anything in the way of pebbles or shells to bring home for her Memory Book. She danced down the Other Stairs, kissed Grandma good-by, and picking up her basket for the ferns, ran merrily off.

Molly was waiting for her, and together they trotted down the sandy path to the boathouse. It had rained the day before and the path was a bit muddy, but with heavy shoes the children did not need rubbers.

"Isn't it warm?" said Molly. "I 'most wish I'd worn a hat, it's so sunny."

"I hate a hat," said Marjorie, "but I'll tell you what, Molly, if we had my red parasol we could hold it over our heads."

"Just the thing, Mopsy; do skip back and get it. I'll hold your basket, and Carter isn't here yet."

Marjorie ran back as fast as she could, pattering along the muddy path and thinking only of the red parasol, bounded in at the front door and up the Front Stairs!

Grandma was in the upper hall, and her heart sank as she saw the child, thoughtlessly unconscious of wrongdoing, clatter up the stairs, her heavy boots splashing mud and wet on every polished step.

Her heart sank, not so much because of the mud on the steps as because of this new proof of Marjorie's thoughtlessness.

"My dear little girl!" she said, as Marjorie reached the top step, and in a flash Marjorie realized what she had done.

Crestfallen and horrified, she threw herself into her grandmother's arms.

"I'm sorry, Midget dear, but I cannot break my word. You know what I told you."

"Yes, Grandma, and I am so sorry, but please, oh, Grandma
dear,—can't you just postpone the punishment till to-morrow? 'Cause
Molly and I are going to Blossom Banks to dig ferns, and it's such a
BEAUTIFUL day for ferns."
Grandma Sherwood hesitated. It almost broke her heart to deprive the child of her holiday,
and yet it was for Marjorie's own good that an attempt must be made to cure her of her
carelessness.

"No, Marjorie; I cannot postpone the punishment until to-morrow. If you wanted to go
rowing to-day, you should have waited to run up these stairs until to-morrow. You didn't
postpone your naughtiness, so I cannot postpone its punishment."

Marjorie looked dumfounded. She had not intended to be naughty, but also she had never
supposed her gentle grandma could be so severe. She looked utterly disconsolate, and said in
despairing tones: "But, Grandma, won't you let me go rowing this morning and give me the
punishment this afternoon? I must go; Molly and Carter are down by the boathouse waiting
for me! Please, Grandma!"

So difficult was it for Mrs. Sherwood to resist the child's pleading tones that her own voice
was more stern than she intended to make it, lest she reveal her true feeling.

"No, Marjorie; you have been very naughty now, and so you must be punished now. Listen
to me. I shall send Jane to tell Carter to go back to his work and to tell Molly to go home.
I'm sorry to spoil your pleasure, but remember you have really spoiled it yourself."

Marjorie did not cry, she was not that sort of a child. But she had a broken-down, wilted air,
the very despondency of which almost made her grandmother relent. Had it been a more
important occasion she might have done so, but the children could go on the river any day,
and though it was a very real disappointment to Marjorie to stay at home, yet discipline
required it.

"Now, Marjorie," went on Mrs. Sherwood, after Jane had been despatched on her errand,
"take off those muddy shoes and set them on the top step of the stairs."

Rather wondering at this command, Marjorie sat down on the top step, unlaced her shoes,
and did with them as she had been bidden.

"Now, this is your punishment, my child; you came up these stairs when you had been told
not to do so: now you may spend the rest of the day on the stairs. You are not to leave them
until six o'clock to-night. With the muddy steps and your muddy shoes in front of your eyes
all day long, you may, perhaps, learn to remember better in future."

Marjorie could scarcely believe her ears. To stay on the stairs all day long seemed a funny punishment; and except for missing the row on the river, it did not seem a very hard one.

"May I have a book, Grandma," she asked, still a little bewildered by the outlook.

Grandma considered. "Yes," she said at last; "you may go to your room, put on your worsted bedroom slippers, and then you may bring back with you any books or toys you care for."

"How many?" asked Marjorie, whose spirits were rising, for her punishment seemed to promise a novel experience.

"As many as you can carry at once," replied Grandma, turning aside to hide a smile.

In a few minutes Marjorie returned. She had turned up the short, full skirt of her pink gingham frock to form a sort of bag, and into it she had tumbled, helter-skelter, several books, some paper and pens, her paper-doll's house, her paintbox, her kitten, a few odd toys, her Memory Book, and her clock. Staggering under the bulging load, but in a more cheerful frame of mind, she reached the stairs again.

"I brought my clock," she observed, "because I shall want to know as the hours so by; but I'll be careful not to scratch the stairs with it, Grandma."

"Your carefulness comes too late, Marjorie. I shall have to send for a man from town to repolish the stairs, anyway, for the nails in the heels of your heavy boots have entirely ruined them."

"Oh, Grandma, I am so sorry; and if you think a day won't be punishment enough, I'll stay for a week. Do I get anything to eat?" she added, as a sudden thought of their picnic luncheon occurred to her. "You might just send me the picnic basket."

"Jane will bring you your dinner," said her grandmother, shortly, for she began to think the punishment she had devised was more like a new game.

"Goody!" cried Marjorie. "I do love dinner on a tray. Send plenty of strawberries, please; and, Grandma, don't think that I'm not truly being punished, for I am. I shall think over my naughtiness a good deal, and when I look at those awful shoes, I don't see how I COULD have done such a wicked thing. But you know yourself, Grandma, that we ought to make the best of everything, and so I'll just get what fun I can out of my books and my strawberries."

Mrs. Sherwood went away, uncertain whether she had succeeded in what she had intended to do or not. She knew Marjorie would not leave the stairs without permission, for the little girl was exceedingly conscientious.

Left to herself, Marjorie began to take in the situation.

She carefully unpacked her dressful of things, and arranged them on the steps. In this she became greatly interested. It was a novel way of living, to go always up and down and never sideways. She planned her home for the day with care and thought. She decided to reserve a narrow space next the banister to go up and down; and to arrange her belongings on the other side of the staircase. She put her clock on the top step that she might see it from any point of view; and on the other steps she laid neatly her books, her paint-box, her writing things, and her toys. She became absorbed in this occupation, and delightedly scrambled up and down, arranging and rearranging her shelved properties.

"It's a good deal like my shelf in my own room," she thought, "except it's all in little pieces instead of straight ahead. But that doesn't really matter, and I'm not sure but I like it better this way. Now, I think I'll write a letter to Mother, first, and confess this awful thing I've done. I always feel better after I get my confessions off of my mind, and when Jane brings my dinner I expect she'll take it to be mailed."

Marjorie scrambled up to a step near the top where her little writing tablet was. She arranged her paper and took up her pen, only to discover that in her haste she had forgotten to bring any ink.

"But it doesn't matter," she thought, cheerfully, "for it would have upset in my dress probably, and, anyway, I can just as well use a pencil."

But the pencil's point was broken, and, of course, it had not occurred to her to bring a knife. She had promised Grandma not to leave the stairs without permission, so there was nothing to do but to give up the idea of letter-writing, and occupy herself with something else.

"And, anyway," she thought, "it must be nearly dinner time, for I've been here now for hours and hours."

She glanced at the clock, and found to her amazement that it was just twenty minutes since her grandmother had left her alone.

"The clock must have stopped!" she said, bending her ear to listen.

But it hadn't, and Marjorie suddenly realized that a whole day, solitary and alone, is an interminable length of time.

"Oh, dear," she sighed, putting her head down on her arms on the step above, "I do wish I had gone up the Other Stairs! This day is going to last forever! I just know it is! But if it ever DOES get over, I never want to see the Front Stairs again!"

CHAPTER X
A LONG DAY
Marjorie had expected to derive much satisfaction, during her sojourn on the stairs, from playing with her kitten. But Puff ran away almost immediately, and no amount of calling or coaxing could bring her back.

Sighing deeply, Marjorie tried to amuse herself reading the books she had brought. But the light was not very good on the stairs, and somehow, too, the books seemed to have lost their interest. Thinking over what she could do to make the time pass, she remembered her paintbox. She was fond of painting, and concluded she would try to paint a little sketch of the stairs to put in her Memory Book to represent this dreadful day.

"Not that I need anything to make me remember it," she thought, "for I'm sure I can never, never, never forget it." But when she had her other materials all prepared she realized she had no glass of water, so, of course, her paints were useless.

Even her paper-doll's house seemed to have lost its flavor. She had no new things to paste in, nor had she any paste.

She began to learn what a lot of little things make up the comforts of life, and, utterly discouraged, she tried to think of something to while away the time.

At last she concluded she would start at the top and go down, sitting on each step five minutes. "This," she calculated to herself, "will fill up a long time. There are seventeen steps, and seventeen times five is,—well, I don't know how much it is, exactly, but it must be several hours. Perhaps, when I get down to the bottom it will be afternoon!"

With a reviving sense of interest in something, she sat on the top step and waited for five minutes to pass. Never had a period of time seemed so long. It was twice as long as a church service, and a dozen times as long as the ride in the cars when she came up to Grandma's. But at last the five minutes was up, and with a little jounce Marjorie slid down to the next step, and prepared to spend another five. This was longer yet, and at the third-step Marjorie gave up this plan, as being the most dreadful thing she had ever tried.

She began to feel like crying, but was determined not to do anything so foolish.

Slowly and wearily the morning dragged away, and at last, when Marjorie had begun to feel that lassitude which comes from utter weariness, Jane appeared with a tray of luncheon.

Marjorie brightened up at once. "Oh, Jane," she cried, "I'm SO glad to see you! I AM so lonesome!"

"Pore lamb!" said Jane, sympathetically; "I'm thinkin' ye're purty nigh dead, be now. But here's the foine lunch for ye. See, darlint, here's chicken and strawberries and jelly and all the things ye like best! Cheer up, now, and ate yer food."

"Indeed, I will! Oh, Jane, what lovely things! Fresh little cakes, with pink icing; and gooseberry jam! But don't go away, Jane."

"I must, Miss Midget. Yer grandma towld me not to shtay wid yez."

"But I'm so lonesome," said Marjorie, who had just seemed to realize what the main trouble was.

But Jane dared not disobey orders, and setting the tray on the stairs, she went away, with fond backward glances at the forlorn little figure sitting there.

However, the lonesomest human heart is bound to cheer up a little under the influence of a specially fine feast, and as Marjorie ate her luncheon and drank a big glass of milk, the detested stairs began to assume a rather more attractive air.

And so, when Jane came to take the tray away she found on it only empty dishes, while Marjorie, who was cuddled up in a corner, reading, looked at her with a smile.

"The day is half gone!" she announced, triumphantly. "And, Jane, won't you ask Grandma if you may bring me a glass of water so I can paint. But tell her I don't want it unless she's perfectly willing."

Grandma smiled a little at the stipulation, but sent Marjorie the glass of water, and the child filled up half an hour or more painting pictures. But the cramped position was very uncomfortable, and Marjorie grew restless and longed for exercise. Suddenly an inspiration seized her, and she concluded it would be great fun to slide down the banister. For a few times this was amusing, but it stung her hands, and finally she fell off and bumped her head rather soundly.

"It's lucky I fell on the stair side," she said to herself, rubbing the lump on her forehead, "for I promised Grandma not to leave the stairs, and if I had fallen off on the other side I should have broken my promise!"

The afternoon hours seemed to move rather more slowly than the morning. Occasionally, Marjorie's naturally cheerful disposition would assert itself and she would bravely endeavor to occupy herself pleasantly in some way. But there was so little light, and stairs are uncomfortable at best to sit on, and the silence and loneliness were so oppressive, that her efforts successively failed.

And, though Marjorie did not realize it, her spirits were depressed because of the mere fact that she was undergoing punishment. Had she been there of her own free choice she could have played happily on the stairs all day long; or had the opportunity been bestowed upon her, as a great and special treat, the hours would have flown by.

At last, exhausted, Nature conquered all else, and, seated on one step, Marjorie folded her arms on the step above, laid her head down upon them, and went to sleep.

And it was thus that Uncle Steve found her when he came home at four o'clock.

"Hello, Queen of Mischief!" he cried, gayly. "Wake up here and tell me all about it!"

"Oh, Uncle Steve!" cried Marjorie, waking, flushed from her nap, and delighted at having some one to speak to; "do you know why I'm here? Did Grandma tell you?"

"Yes, she told me; and she told me something else, too. She says that if you are properly sorry for what you did,—really, AWFULLY sorry, you know,—that you may be excused for the rest of the day and may go out driving with me."

"Well, I just rather guess I AM sorry! I'm two sorries. One, because I disobeyed Grandma and tracked up her Front Stairs; and another, because I've had this terrible, dreadful punishment."

Uncle Steve looked at his niece a little gravely. "Which are you more sorry for, Marjorie," he asked: "because you did wrong or because you were punished?"

Marjorie considered. "About equal, I think. No, I'm more sorry I did wrong, because if I hadn't, I wouldn't have had the punishment; and, besides, it hurt Grandma's feelings."

"Which did?"

"Why, my running up the stairs! Of course, the punishment didn't hurt her," and Marjorie laughed merrily at the idea.

"I think it hurt her more than it did you," said Uncle Steve, but Marjorie only stared, open-eyed, at this nonsense.
"Well, anyway, it's all over now; so bundle your belongings back where they belong and get yourself ready for a drive."

Marjorie flew to obey, but meeting Grandma in the hall, she dropped her dressful of books and toys, and flung herself into Mrs. Sherwood's waiting arms.

"Oh, Grandma!" she cried. "I AM so sorry I slam-banged upstairs, and I'll never do it again, and I had a perfectly awful, DREADFUL time, but of course you had to punish me for your own good,—I mean for my own good,—but now it's all over, and you love me just the same, don't you?"

The ardent embrace in progress left no doubt of the affection still existing between the pair, and if Marjorie's hugs were of the lovingly boisterous variety, Grandma Sherwood appeared quite willing to submit to them.

"I don't know," she thought to herself, after Marjorie had gone for her drive, "whether that child is impervious to discipline or whether she is unusually capable of receiving and assimilating it."

But at any rate, Marjorie never went up or down the front stairs again, except on the occasions when it was distinctly permissible.

The drive with Uncle Steve was a succession of delights. This was partly because it was such a sudden and pleasant change from the abominable staircase and partly because Uncle Steve was such an amiable and entertaining companion.

The two were alone in an old-fashioned, low basket-phaeton; and Uncle Steve was willing to stop whenever Marjorie wished, to note an especially beautiful bird on a neighboring branch or an extra-fine blossom of some wild flower.

Also, Uncle Steve seemed to know the names of all the trees and flowers and birds they chanced to see. Greatly interested in these things, Marjorie learned much nature-lore, and the lessons were but play. Tying the horse to a fence, the two cronies wandered into the wood and found, after much careful search, some Indian Pipes of an exquisite perfection. These fragile, curious things were Marjorie's great delight, and she carried them carefully home for her Memory Book.

"They won't be very satisfactory as mementoes," warned Uncle Steve, "for they will turn brown and lose their fair, white beauty."

Marjorie looked regretful, but an inspiration came to her.

"I'll tell you what, Uncle Steve, I'll get Stella to draw them in my book and paint them. She's so clever at copying flowers, and I'm sure she can do it."

"Let her try it, then, and if she doesn't succeed I'll photograph them for you, so you'll have at least a hint of the lovely things."

Hand in hand they walked through the wood, spying new beauties here and there. Sometimes they sat on a fallen log to rest a bit or to discuss some new marvel in Nature's kingdom.

At last, as the sun was sinking low in the west, they left the wood, untied old Betsy, who was patiently waiting for them, and jogged along homeward.

"Punishment is a strange thing," said Marjorie to Grandma, as they were having their little "twilight talk" that evening, before the child went to bed.

"Why?" asked Grandma.

"Because it makes you remember," said Marjorie, slowly; "I don't see why I couldn't remember to keep off the Front Stairs, just because you told me to, but somehow I couldn't. Now, after to-day, I'm sure I shall never forget again."

"That's the difference, my child, between youth and age. You are young and careless of other people's wishes. I want you to learn to consider others before yourself, and to remember to do so without a dreadful punishment to fix it in your memory."

"It's lucky, isn't it, that I don't get punished for all the naughty things I do? It would keep me busy being punished most of the time."

"You ARE a mischievous child, Marjorie; but your mischief is always the result of carelessness or forgetfulness. I have never known you purposely to disobey me or deliberately to cut up some naughty trick."

"No, I don't, Grandma; often I'm being just as good as an angel and as quiet as a mouse, when suddenly something pops into my head that would be fun to do; and I fly and do it, before I think, and just about every time it's something wrong!"

"Then suppose you try to act more slowly. When you think of some piece of fun, pause a moment, to make sure that it isn't mischief. There's quite enough innocent fun in the world to keep you busy all day, and every day."

"I 'spect there is; and truly, Grandma, after this, when I want to cut up jinks, I'll wait until I can think it out, whether they're good jinks or bad jinks! Will that do?"

"That will do admirably," said Grandma, smiling as she kissed the little girl; "if you go through life on that principle and if you have judgment enough—and I think you have—to tell 'good jinks' from 'bad jinks,' you will probably have plenty of good times without any necessity for punishment."

"Then that's all right," said Marjorie, and feeling that her life problems were all settled, she dropped off to sleep.

CHAPTER XI
THE DUNNS
"Marjorie," said Mrs. Sherwood, one morning, "do you know where Mrs. Dunn lives?"
"Yes, Grandma; down the river-road, toward the blacksmith's."

"Yes, that's right; and I wish you would go down there for me and carry a small basket. There isn't any one else I can send this morning and I have just heard that she is quite ill."

"They're awfully poor people, aren't they? Are you sending them something nice?"

"Yes; some food. Mrs. Dunn scalded her hands severely last night, and I fear she will not be able to work for several days. So if you will carry them these things for their dinner, I will try to get down there myself this afternoon."

"Of course I will, Grandma; I'm glad to help the poor people. May I ask Molly to go with me?"
"Why, yes; I don't care. If there are two of you, you can carry more things. Run over after her, and I'll have the baskets ready by the time you get back."

With a hop and a skip, Marjorie took the shortcut across the fields to Molly's house. It was a beautiful summer morning, and Marjorie didn't stop more than half a dozen times, to watch the crows or the bees or the clouds or a hop-toad.

She captured Molly, and after waiting for that dishevelled young person to scramble into a clean frock, the two girls hopped and skipped back again.

Marjorie was somewhat inexperienced in the practical matters of charity, and looked with surprise at the large quantity of substantial viands.

"There is a large family of the Dunns," observed Grandma, "and they're all blessed with healthy appetites. These things won't go to waste."

"Are there children?" asked Marjorie.

"Yes, indeed, four of them. You must see how Mrs. Dunn is and find out if she's badly hurt. Ask her what she wants especially, and tell her I am coming this afternoon, and I'll carry it to her."

The girls trotted away with the well-filled baskets, and Grandma Sherwood looked after them a little uncertainly, as she saw how preoccupied they were in their own conversation, and remembered how careless Marjorie was, and how prone to mischief.

"Thim scalawags'll be afther havin' a picnic wid thim baskets," prophesied Eliza, as she too watched the children's departure.

Grandma Sherwood laughed. "I hardly think they'll do that," she said; "but they're liable to set down the baskets, and go hunting for wild flowers or something, and never think of their errand again."

But, on the contrary, the children were quite interested in their mission.

"Your grandma is an awful good woman," observed Molly.

"Yes, she is," agreed Marjorie, "it's lovely of her to send all these good things to poor people. It must be awful to be so poor that you don't have enough to eat!"

"Yes, but it must be lovely when the baskets come in."

"But they don't always come in," said Marjorie.

"They must," declared Molly, with an air of conviction; "if they didn't, the poor people would have nothing to eat, and then they would die; and you know yourself, we never hear of anybody dying of starvation around here."

"No; not around here, maybe. But in China they drop off by millions, just from starvation."

"Well, they wouldn't if your grandmother was there. She'd send baskets to every one of them."

"I believe she would," said Marjorie, laughing; "she'd manage it somehow."

By this time they had reached the Dunns' domain. At least they had come to a broken-down gate in a tumble-down fence, which Marjorie knew was the portal of their destination. In their endeavors to open the rickety gate the girls pushed it over, and nearly fell over, themselves.

But carefully holding their baskets they climbed over the pile of fallen pickets and followed the grass-grown path to the house.

And a forlorn enough house it was. Everything about it betokened not only poverty but shiftlessness. Marjorie was not experienced enough to know how often the former is the result of the latter, and her heart was full of pity for people who must live in such comfortless surroundings. The little old cottage was unpainted, and the front porch was in such a dilapidated condition that one step was entirely missing and several floor-boards were gone.

"It's like walking a tight-rope," said Marjorie, as she picked her way carefully along what she hoped was a sound plank. "But it's rather exciting. I wonder if we can get in."

There was no bell, and she tapped loudly on the door.

Almost instantly it was opened by a child whose appearance almost made Marjorie scream out with laughter.
A little girl of about ten, dressed in a bright pink skirt and a bright blue waist, stood before them. This startling color combination was enhanced by a red sash, which, though faded in streaks, was wide and tied at the back in a voluminous bow. The girl's naturally straight hair had apparently been urged by artificial means to curl in ringlets, but only a part of it had succumbed to the hot iron. The rest fairly bristled in its stiff straightness, and the whole mop was tied up with a large bow of red ribbon.

This rainbow-hued specimen of humanity opened the door with a flourish and bowed to the visitors with an air of extreme elegance.

Marjorie looked at her in astonishment. The gorgeous trappings and the formal demeanor of the child made her think she must have mistaken the house.

"Is this Mrs. Dunn's house?" she inquired, with some hesitation.

"Yes; I'm Miss Dunn," said the child, with such a ridiculous air of affectation that Molly giggled outright.

"Yes," Miss Dunn went on, "I am the eldest daughter. My name is Ella.
They call me the Elegant Ella, but I don't mind."
"I am Marjorie Maynard and Mrs. Sherwood is my grandmother. She heard your mother was ill and she sent her these baskets."

"How kind of her!" exclaimed the Elegant Ella, clasping her hands and rolling up her eyes. "Won't you come in?"

As Marjorie and Molly had been with difficulty balancing themselves on the broken boards of the porch, they were glad to accept the invitation.

Their first glance at the interior of the cottage showed that the rest of the family and the ways of the house did not at all harmonize with the manner and appearance of the eldest daughter.

Everything was of the poorest, and there was no attempt at order or thrift.

Mrs. Dunn sat in a rockerless rocking-chair, her left hand wrapped in bandages and her right hand holding a book which she was reading.

As the girls entered she threw the book on the floor and smiled at them pleasantly.

"Walk right in," she said, "and take seats if you can find any. Hoopsy Topsy, get off that chair this minute and give it to the ladies! Dibbs, you lift Plumpy out of the other one, quick! There! Now you girls set down and rest yourselves! Did you bring them baskets for us? Lawsee! What a good woman Mis' Sherwood is, to be sure! Now ain't that just like her! She's so kind and gen'rous-hearted that she makes it a pleasure fer folks to get all scalted with hot water! Ella, you fly round and empty them baskets so's the young ladies can take them home again. But you set a while, girls, and visit."

"Are you much hurt, Mrs. Dunn?" asked Marjorie. "And how did it happen?"

"Hurt! Land sakes, I guess I am! Why, the hull kittle of boilin' water just doused itself on my hand and foot!"

"That's why Ma didn't rise to greet you," explained the Elegant Ella, and again Molly had hard work to keep her face straight as she noted the girl's comical efforts at etiquette.

"Aw, you keep still, Ella," said her mother; "you ain't got no call to talk to the young ladies."

But although Mrs. Dunn apparently tried to subdue her elegant daughter, yet it was plain to be seen that she greatly admired the flower of the family, and spoke thus merely from a pretended modesty.

"Ella's so fond of dress," said Mrs. Dunn, "that she jest don't hev time to bother with housekeepin'. So Hoopsy Topsy does it, and that's why we ain't so slick as we might be. But fer a child of eight, I must say Hoopsy Topsy does wonderful well."

Mrs. Dunn's pride in her offspring was unmistakable, and Hoopsy Topsy, who quite understood she was being complimented, smiled and looked happily self-conscious.

The novelty of the scene quite fascinated Marjorie. She had expected that abject poverty would leave its victims a despondent, down-hearted set of people; and instead of that she found them not only pleasant and amiable, but seemingly happy and care-free.

"My grandmother said, Mrs. Dunn," said Marjorie, "that if you would tell me of anything you specially want she would come this afternoon and bring it to you."

"My! ain't she good!" said Mrs. Dunn. "Well, if she don't mind, I'd like some old linen to wrap around the burns. You see, I am scalted pretty bad and it'll be a while 'fore I kin get to work again. But, of course, the children are right handy, an' ef we jest have a stove an' a bed we can scratch along somehow. Ella, she's more hifalutin. She'd like red plush sofys and lace curtings. But I say, 'Land, child! What's the use of worrying? If you can't have them things, you can't!' So, Ella, she makes the best of what she has, and I must say she does have wonderful fine taste."

Marjorie looked at the Elegant Ella, and, though she didn't agree with Mrs. Dunn as to Ella's taste, she felt sorry for the poor child, who wanted the refinements of life, yet was doomed to live without them.

"It is of no consequence," said Ella, tossing her head; "we are very comfortable; and though I should like a piano, I am in no haste to procure one."

"Lucky you ain't," observed her mother, "as I don't see none runnin' this way. What's the matter, Dibbsy dear?"

Dibbs, who was a baby of four years, was sitting on the floor digging both his fists into his eyes. And though not audibly crying, he evidently was not entirely happy.

"Wants to know what's in de bastick!" he announced without hesitation.

"So you shall," declared his fond mother. "Hoopsy Topsy, lift Dibbs up so he can see what the young ladies brought."

Nothing loath, Hoopsy Topsy lifted up her brother, who at once forgot his grief, and, smiling broadly, began to investigate the baskets.

"Land sake, Ella," said Mrs. Dunn, "I told you to empty them baskets long ago. Whatever have you been a-doin' all this time?"

"I was retying my sash, Ma," exclaimed Ella, reappearing from the next room; "I think it has more of an air tied on the side."

"Ain't she the airy piece!" exclaimed the proud mother, looking at her daughter with undisguised admiration.

But it seemed to Molly and Marjorie that, if anything could be funnier than the Ella who first met them, it was the Ella of the retied sash!

Having arranged her finery to her satisfaction, Ella proceeded with her work of taking the things from the baskets, and, as she lifted out a large piece of cold beef, a delicious pie, some tea and sugar, and various parcels of bread and butter, and a jar of apple-sauce, the little Dunns all gathered round, quite unable to refrain from noisy expressions of glee and delight.

"Jiminy Christmas!" cried Hoopsy Topsy, quite upsetting Dibbs as she made a rush for the pie. And then Plumpy, the baby, wiggled his fat little self across the floor and joined the crowd about the pie, and aided by the Elegant Ella, in a few moments there wasn't any pie at all.

"Just look at them," said Mrs. Dunn, placidly; "you'd think they didn't have no manners! But they're that fond of pie, you wouldn't believe! They don't never get none, you know, and so it's a novelty."

"We'd like it if we had it every day," announced Hoopsy Topsy, with her mouth full.

"Pie ev'y day!" agreed Dibbs, as he contentedly munched his piece. The whole scene made a great impression on the two visitors, but they were affected quite differently. Marjorie felt a strong inclination to get away as soon as she could, for, though she felt very sorry for the poor people and was glad to give them things, yet the situation was not at all attractive, and having done her errand, she was quite ready to go.

Not so Molly. That active and energetic young person was dismayed at the untidiness and discomfort all about, and felt a strong desire at least to alleviate it.

"Mrs. Dunn," she said, "of course with your injured hand and foot you can't sweep. Mayn't I just take a broom and brush up a little? You'd be so much more comfortable."

"Land sakes, child, 'taint fer you to be sweepin' our house! Ella here, she can sweep; and Hoopsy Topsy's a good fist at it."

"I shall tidy up the room to-morrow," said Ella, with an air of haughty apology, "but to-day I have a hat to trim and I can't be bothered with household matters."

"Ella's just great on trimmin' hats," observed her mother, "and Mis' Green, she giv' her her last year's straw; and Ella, she'll trim it up so Mis' Green herself couldn't recognize it!"

Marjorie didn't doubt this in the least, and as Molly's suggestion had put an idea into her own head, she began to look upon an acquaintance with the Dunns as a new sort of entertainment.

CHAPTER XII
THE BAZAAR

"Mrs. Dunn," Marjorie said, "please let Molly and me fix up this room a little bit. Now, I'll tell you what: you and the children take these baskets of things out into the kitchen and put them away, or eat them, or do what you please. And then you all stay out there until we tell you you may come back. Ella can trim her hat if she chooses, and Hoopsy Topsy can take care of the children, and you can go on with your reading which we interrupted."

"Now, ain't you kind," said Mrs. Dunn; "I do declare that would be jest lovely! I ain't had a good rest like that in I don't know when! Hoopsy Topsy, you and Ella'll have to shove me out in this here chair. I can hobble some, but I can't walk."

With the children's assistance, Mrs. Dunn was transferred to the other room, her children followed, and Midge and Molly were left to their own devices.

"It's hopeless," said Marjorie, as she looked around at the untidy room.

"Not a bit of it!" declared Molly; "if I only had a decent broom instead of this old stub! Now, I'll sweep, Mopsy, and you find something that'll do for a duster, and we'll straighten up the place in less than no time."

Molly was a brave little housekeeper, and though Marjorie knew less about it, she was an apt pupil, and the whole performance seemed great fun. In less than an hour the two girls had quite transformed the room. Everything was clean and tidy, and Marjorie had scampered out and picked a bunch of daisies and clover to decorate the mantel.

"They haven't any pretty things," she said, as she scowled at the effect of her bouquet in an old cracked jar. "I'll tell you what, Molly, let's come back to-morrow and bring some little traps to decorate with. I can spare a number of things out of my own room; and Grandma will give me some, I know; and Uncle Steve will give me some, too."

"Yes, I can bring a lot," said Molly, with enthusiasm; "let's make this family all over. Let's make them be neat and tidy and thrifty."

"Do you suppose we can?" said Marjorie, doubtfully.

"Well, we can try," said Molly. "Now let's call them in, and then let's go home. It must be dinner-time, and I'm nearly starved."

They opened the door and found the Dunn family apparently happy and contented; and in no wise disturbed by the unusual occupation of their visitors.

"Come in," cried Marjorie, "come in all of you, and see how nice your room looks!"

"I can't come just now," said Elegant Ella, whose speech was rather indistinct by reason of several pins held in her mouth. "I'm trimming my hat, and if I leave it now I'll forget how I was going to arrange the feather."

"I think I won't move just at present," said Mrs. Dunn. "The gettin' out here hurt me more'n I thought it was goin' to, and now I'm landed, I guess I'll set a spell. I'm ever so much obliged to you fer all your kindness, and now you'd better run along home or your grandma'll be worried. You're mighty good children, and I'm glad to have that room swep' up; it must be a weight off en Ella's mind."

It did not seem probable that Ella ever had a weight on her mind in the way of housekeeping cares, but at the moment she was so absorbed in her hat-trimming that she paid no attention to her mother's remark.

It seemed hard that Molly and Midge had no one to appreciate the results of their labors, but Hoopsy Topsy was washing the dishes after the family meal, Plumpy was asleep on the floor, and Dibbs was playing out in the door-yard, with some battered old toys.

So, taking their baskets, Molly and Midge started homeward.

"I thought it would be fun to take things to poor people," said Marjorie, with an air of disappointment; "but those people are too aggravating for anything. They just accept what you bring and hardly thank you for it, and then they seem to want you to go home as fast as you can."

"That's so," agreed Molly; "but I don't care whether they like it or not. I think we ought to try to do them good. I don't mean only to take them things to eat, but try to make them more—more—"

"Respectable," suggested Marjorie. "But I suppose that Ella thinks she's more respectable than we are this minute."

"I s'pose she does; but we oughtn't to be discouraged by such things. I think mother'll give me some of my last year's dresses to give her, and then she won't have to wear that funny-looking rig she had on."

"She likes that," said Marjorie. "I don't believe she'd wear your dresses if you took them to her."

By this time the girls had reached the Sherwood house, and Grandma invited Molly to stay to dinner, which invitation the little girl gladly accepted.

At the dinner-table they told Grandma the whole story of the morning.

Mrs. Sherwood was greatly amused at their description of the Dunn family, and greatly surprised to learn of their efforts in the house-cleaning line.

"I want you to be charitable," she said, "and generously inclined toward the poor and needy. But I don't want you to adopt such unusual methods of dispensing your charity. After this, when you feel inclined to such energetic measures, come home first and ask permission. Then, if the plan seems to me feasible, you can carry it out."

"But, Grandma," said Marjorie, "the Dunns really need help. They can't seem to do anything and they haven't anything to do with."

"But you're too young, my child, to know what they do need. You must be content to help them under the direction of some one older than yourself. Mrs. Dunn, I fear, is not a thrifty or hard-working woman. She has not been here long, and I know little about her; but I've been told that she quite spoils that oldest child and makes the second one do all the work."

"The second one is named Hoopsy Topsy," said Marjorie, laughing; "and she's like her name. She's always tumbling down and racing about, with her dress torn and her hair in her eyes, like a perfect witch. The Elegant Ella is quite different. Truly, Grandma, they're a funny lot, and if you go there this afternoon, mayn't we go with you?"

"No," said Mrs. Sherwood, "I shall go by myself, to-day, and investigate the case. Perhaps some other time I may take you children."

The girls were disappointed, but when they found they couldn't go, they went out to Marjorie's porch to talk it all over.

"I think," said Marjorie, "it's our duty to do something for those children. Just think, Molly, we have everything we want, and they have nothing."

"I'll tell you what, Mopsy: let's sew and make things for them; dresses, you know, and aprons."

"I can't sew fit to be seen, Molly; and 'twould take me all summer to get one apron made. I'd rather give them things that we have. Why, I'd rather give Ella my best parasol than to try to sew anything for her!"

"Oh, don't give her that lovely parasol! We'll think of something else. Suppose we invite them all to dinner; you one day, and I another."

"I don't believe Grandma would like that. And, anyway, that would only give them dinner for two days; we couldn't keep it up, you know. But, Molly, I'll tell you what! Let's have a fair, or a bazaar or something,—and make some money for them that way."

"Just the thing! That would be lovely. Where shall we have it?"

"Right here in this porch. Uncle Steve'll help, I know. And I'm sure Grandma won't mind our doing that."

When Marjorie laid the plan before Mrs. Sherwood that lady quite approved of it.

"Now, that's something sensible," she said; "it will be very nice for you girls to make things, and have a pretty little fair, but don't go down there again and sweep rooms for those people. I'm very sorry for poor Mrs. Dunn, but in this neighborhood there are not many poor people, and as the farmers are all kind-hearted I do not think she will suffer for lack of food while her injuries keep her from her work."

"Isn't there any Mr. Dunn?" asked Marjorie.

"No; he died a few months ago. That is why she had to come here and live in that forlorn little cottage. She hopes to support herself and her children by going out to work each day, but until her burns get well of course she can't do that."

"I'm sorry for her," said Marjorie, decidedly, "and I hope we'll make a lot at our fair to help her along."

When they told Stella about the plan for the fair, she thought it all great fun. She did not seem to care much about the Dunns or their needs, and positively refused to visit the little old cottage, but she was ready to work for the fair with all her might.

There seemed to be no end to the pretty things Stella knew how to make. She was a clever little artist, and she painted cards, pictures, and trinkets of all sorts, which Molly and Midge helped to make up into various salable fancy articles.

Midge was ingenious, too, and every afternoon the three worked busily, making all sorts of things.

Dolls were a specialty; and they made funny Chinese-looking affairs by stringing peanuts together, and making queer little costumes out of Japanese paper-napkins. They made paper dolls, too, which Stella painted prettily, and they dressed some little china dolls and wooden Dutch dolls.

Uncle Steve brought them materials to make up; and a letter which Marjorie wrote to her mother resulted in the arrival of a big box filled with all sorts of pretty and curious things, which would doubtless find a ready sale.

Marjorie crocheted mats and strung bead chains, while Molly, whose tastes were practical, made sweeping-caps and ironing-holders by the dozen.

So enthusiastic did the girls grow over their plan that their elders became interested, and soon donations for the fair began to arrive from many of the neighbors.

As the day drew near, preparations went on more rapidly, and the affair took on larger proportions.

It was arranged that all the toys, dolls, and fancy things for sale should be displayed in Marjorie's porch. Carter had put up some long tables, which Grandma Sherwood had draped prettily with white and light green cheese-cloth.

The other parts of the big veranda were arranged with tables, where ices and cakes were to be served; and a pretty booth was devoted to the sale of home-made candies.

The verandas and grounds were made gay with flags and Chinese lanterns. Uncle Steve superintended these decorations, which insured their being beautiful and appropriate. A tent on the lawn sheltered some musicians; and in an arbor, lemonade was dispensed.

The day of the bazaar was clear and pleasant, and not too warm. Early in the afternoon, Stella and Molly arrived, and the two, with Midge, all in their fresh white dresses, flitted about from one booth to another, to make sure that everything was in readiness.

Several other girls and boys, and some ladies and gentlemen too, had been invited to assist in selling the things and to wait on the guests, so that when the bazaar opened at four o'clock in the afternoon a merry lot of young people were scattered about the grounds.

Marjorie was in her element. "Oh, Uncle Steve," she cried; "isn't it all perfectly lovely! And I think we'll make quite a lot of money, don't you?"

"I do, indeed, Mopsy. I'm only afraid, by the way the customers are flocking in, that we haven't provided enough refreshment for them."

And sure enough, though the hour was yet early, crowds of people were coming in at the gate.

The fame of the little fair had spread among the country people, and they all seemed determined to help along the good cause. Molly and Marjorie found their stock of wares rapidly fading away, while Stella, who was selling lemonade, could scarcely keep enough on hand to supply her customers.

"You must put up your prices, Mopsy," said her uncle; "that's the way to do when your stock is getting low."

61

So Marjorie doubled the price of everything she had left for sale, but even then the dolls and trinkets were willingly bought.

"What shall we do?" said Grandma, in despair. "It isn't seven o'clock, we haven't lighted the lanterns yet for the evening, and the ice cream is all gone! I never dreamed we'd have such a crowd."

"We'll light the lanterns, anyway," declared Uncle Steve, "for if the ice cream is gone they'll want to buy the lanterns next!"

And sure enough they did. When the people came in the evening and learned that everything was sold out but the lanterns, they declared they would buy them for souvenirs. So the merry guests walked about the grounds, carrying the lighted lanterns they had bought (at astonishing prices), and it lent a fantastic effect to the scene to see the lanterns bobbing about among the trees and shrubs on the lawn.

Marjorie was so sorry not to have wares to offer her would-be customers that she ran up to her room several times, gathering up books, pictures, or toys that she thought she could by any possibility spare. She would fly with them down to the porch, mark them at exorbitant prices, and in a few moments they would be sold to the amiable and generous buyers.

It was an unusual experience for a fancy fair, as often there are many unsold wares left to be auctioned off or sold at reduced rates.

When it was all over and the last guests had departed, swinging their lanterns, Marjorie, very tired but very happy, displayed a well-filled cash-box.

"How much do you suppose?" she cried gayly to Uncle Steve.

"Fifty dollars," guessed that jovial gentleman.

"Nonsense," cried Marjorie, "you know there's more than that! But I rather think you'll be surprised when I tell you that there's a little over two hundred dollars!"

"Fine!" exclaimed Uncle Steve. "That will keep the Elegant Ella in fans and sashes for some time!"

"Indeed, it won't be used for that," declared Marjorie. "We're going to give it to Grandma and let her use it for the Dunns just as she thinks best. Little girls can have a fair and earn the money, but it takes older people to manage the rest of it."

"That's true enough, Midge," said Grandma, "but you certainly shall have a share in the pleasure of bestowing it upon our poor neighbors."

CHAPTER XIII
A BIRTHDAY
"Mopsy," said Uncle Steve one morning, "I understand that next week

Thursday has the honor of being your birthday."
"Yes, Uncle Steve, and I'll be twelve years old."

"My gracious goodness! What an old lady you are getting to be! Well, now for such an occasion as that we must celebrate in some way. So I'm going to give you a choice of pleasures. Would you rather have a party, a picnic, or a present?"

Marjorie considered. She well knew that a present which would balance against a party or a picnic would be a fine present, indeed. And so, after a moment's thought, she replied:

"I'll take the present, thank you, Uncle Steve; for somehow I feel sure we'll have picnics this summer, as we always do; and I don't care much about a party, because I know so few children around here."

"All right, then, Midget; a present it shall be, but with this stipulation: you must promise not to go down into the south orchard from now until next Thursday."

"Why not?" asked Mopsy, her eyes wide open with astonishment.

"Principally, because I tell you not to, and I want you to obey me; but I don't mind explaining that it is because I shall be there, at least part of the time, making your present; and as I want it to be a surprise, you mustn't come peeping around."

"All right, Uncle Steve, I won't; but why do you make it down there?
Why not make it up here at the house?"
"Midget, your curiosity will some day get you into trouble. I prefer to do the work in the meadow. Perhaps it is sewing, and I shall take my work-basket and sit under the big maple-trees to sew."

Marjorie laughed to think of Uncle Steve sewing, but was really burning with curiosity to know what he was going to do.

However, she had given her word, and she conscientiously kept it. Not once during those intervening days did she so much as look toward the south meadow, though if she had done so she would not have been able to discover what her birthday surprise was to be.

Every day she discussed the subject with Molly and Stella, and each formed an opinion. Stella thought it was a new flower garden that Uncle Steve was making for Midge; Molly thought he was having a swing put up, because she had seen Carter carrying some long timbers over that way. But the girls considered themselves bound by Mopsy's promise to her uncle, and conscientiously refrained from going down to the meadow to investigate.

Grandma, of course, was in the secret, and as a result she often shut herself into her own room, telling Marjorie she must not come in. She would stay there for hours at a time, and Mopsy felt sure she was sewing on something connected with the birthday surprise, as indeed she was.

As the day came nearer, all the members of the household seemed to be in a state of great excitement. Carter was running about, bringing mysterious-looking parcels from the express office, and taking them to the barn to unpack them.

Eliza was concocting delicious-looking creams and jellies, but they, Marjorie knew, were for the birthday feast, which would, of course, be a hilarious festival, although not a party.

At last Thursday morning came, and Marjorie awoke bright and early; and very soon, arrayed in a fresh, pink gingham frock, went dancing downstairs.

So early was she that the others had not yet come down, and she went out into the kitchen to talk to Eliza.

"Oh, me!" she sighed. "I wish Uncle Steve would hurry. It just seems as if I couldn't wait any longer to know what my birthday surprise is going to be. Do you know, Eliza?"

"Faix, an' I do, Miss Midge, an' it's a foine gift yer uncle has for ye!"

"Don't tell me, Eliza, because Uncle Steve said I mustn't ask questions about it; but do you think I'll like it?"

"'Like it,' is it? 'Deed an' you will thin! Ye'll go crazy as a loonytic wid joy and delight! An' I'm thinkin' you and Miss Molly will be after breaking your necks in it, but the little lady Stella,— I'm feared she won't get in it at all, at all; she'll be too sheared."

"Then it IS a swing," exclaimed Midget, and she felt a little disappointment, for though a swing was lovely to have, yet she had one at home, so it was no especial novelty; and, too, she hadn't thought Uncle Steve would make such a fuss about having a swing built.

"I'm not sayin' it isn't a swing," said Eliza, "and I'm not sayin' it is. And I'm not sayin' it isn't a merry-go-around-about, or whativer ye call thim noisy things that they do be havin' down by the circus tent, and I'm not sayin' it is."

"Don't say any more about what it is or isn't, or I'll guess."

"Indeed you wouldn't, Miss Mopsy, if ye guessed from now until ye're gray-headed."

This made Midget think that the gift was not a swing, as she had already guessed that,—and then she heard Uncle Steve's voice calling her, and she ran gayly back to the dining-room.

The birthday breakfast was a festival indeed. Marjorie's place was decorated with flowers, and even the back of her chair was garlanded with wreaths.

At her plate lay such a huge pile of parcels, tied up in bewitching white papers and gay ribbons, that it seemed as if it would take all day to examine them.

"Goodness me!" exclaimed Midget. "Did anybody ever have so many birthday gifts? Are they all for me?"

"Any that you don't want," said Uncle Steve, "you may hand over to me. I haven't had a birthday for several years now, and I'd be thankful for one small gift."

"You shall have the nicest one here," declared Marjorie, "and I don't care what it is, or who sent it."

"The nicest one isn't here," observed Grandma, with a merry twinkle in her eye, and Marjorie knew that she was thinking of the surprise in the orchard.

"Of course, I mean except the swing," said Marjorie, looking roguishly at Uncle Steve to see if she had guessed right.

"You've been peeping!" he exclaimed, in mock reproach, and then
Marjorie knew that whatever it was, it wasn't a swing.
"You know I haven't—you know I wouldn't," she declared, and then she began to open the lovely-looking bundles.

It did seem as if everybody that Marjorie knew had remembered her birthday. There were gifts from everybody at home, to begin with. Mrs. Maynard had sent the sweetest blue-silk sash, and Mr. Maynard a beautiful book. The children all sent toys or games or trinkets, and every one seemed to Marjorie to be just what she had wanted.

There was a cup and saucer from Eliza, and small tokens from Carter and Jane. For Marjorie was a great pet with the servants, and they all adored her.

But among all the bundles there was no gift from Grandma or Uncle Steve, and Marjorie wondered what had become of the mysterious work which Grandma had been doing all shut up in her own room.

But even as she was thinking about it, Grandma explained:

"Our gifts will come later," she said. "When Uncle Steve gives you his birthday surprise, I will add my contribution."

Just after the last parcel had been untied, Molly and Stella came flying in. That is, Molly came flying, while serious little Stella walked at her usual sedate pace.

"Many happy returns of the day!" cried Molly, "and here's my gift." She had in her arms a large and rather ungainly bundle, loosely wrapped in white tissue paper.

Together she and Marjorie hastily pulled off the papers, and there was a beautiful cat-basket trimmed with blue ribbons and lined with soft cushions for Puff to sleep in.

"Oh!" cried Marjorie, flinging her arms around Molly's neck, "that's just what I've been wanting ever since I've had that kitten." And grabbing up Puff, who was never very far away, she laid her in the basket.

Puff seemed delighted with her new bed, and, after curiously sniffing and poking into all the nooks and corners of it, she curled up and began to purr herself to sleep.

Stella's gift was a dainty, little white-silk parasol, with a frill around it, which seemed to Marjorie the loveliest thing she had ever seen.

"It's beautiful, Stella!" she exclaimed. "And I shall always carry it whenever I'm dressed up enough. I hope you girls will have your birthdays soon, so I can give you some lovely things, too."

"Have you had your surprise yet?" asked impatient Molly, who, according to her usual fashion, was prancing about the room on one foot; while Stella sat demurely in a chair, her hands quietly folded in her lap, though her eyes seemed to make the same inquiry.

"No, not yet," answered Uncle Steve for his niece, "but I think it's about time for us to see if we can find it."

"All right," cried Marjorie, "let's all go to the orchard!"

"I don't see, Midget," said her uncle, "why you think the surprise is down at the orchard, just because I told you I was making it down there. In fact I have my birthday gift for you right here in my pocket."

Marjorie looked rather blank. She knew Uncle Steve loved to tease her, but she had certainly expected some out-of-door gift, and to receive a little trinket that could be carried in a pocket was a surprise indeed.

In proof of his words Uncle Steve drew a neatly-tied parcel from a pocket of his morning coat and handed it to Marjorie. It was about the size of a one-pound box of candy, and sure enough, when Marjorie eagerly pulled off the paper, the gilt letters on the cover proclaimed it a candy-box. Marjorie felt positive that her uncle would not offer her candy as a birthday gift, for he often brought her that on any ordinary day of the year. But she was mystified, and she took off the cover, not knowing herself what she expected to see. To her surprise, inside the box was another parcel, a trifle smaller, and on the paper which wrapped it was written:

"I am not candy as you thought, I bring you joys that can't be bought."

Marjorie began to understand that it was one of Uncle Steve's elaborate jokes, and she didn't know whether further search would reveal a valuable, though tiny gift, or some absurd hoax.

She took out the second box and tore off the wrappings. Molly eagerly helped her pull off the ribbon and paper, and though Stella sat quietly by, she, too, almost held her breath to see what would happen next.

Marjorie opened the second box, and this time was not so much surprised to see that it contained another wrapped and tied box. On this one was written:

"Oho, Miss Mopsy, fooled again! Suppose you keep on trying, then."

"Indeed, I will," cried Mopsy; "I expect there are a thousand boxes, each smaller than the other, and when I get to the end I'll find a bright penny, or something like that!"

"If you think that," said Uncle Steve, "I'll offer you two cents for the bundle as it is now; and then, you see, you'll double your money!"

"No siree!" cried Marjorie, "for, you see, I don't know. It MAY be a diamond ring, but that wouldn't do me much good, as I couldn't wear it until I'm grown up."

"Hurry up," cried Molly, who was dancing about, both helping and hindering Marjorie, "let's see what the next box says."

On the next box was written:

"Just a hint I'll give to you; I'm of metal, tied with blue."

"Metal, tied with blue!" screamed Molly, "What can that be? A hoe, perhaps, tied up with a blue ribbon."

"What kind of a hoe could you get in such a little box?" said Stella.

"I think it's a locket," said Marjorie, "on a blue ribbon to hang round your neck."

The next box said:

"Very seldom you will use me, But you'd cry if you should lose me."

"Ho!" said Marjorie, "if I'm going to use this thing so seldom I don't think I'd cry if I should lose it."

"Perhaps it's a something for Sunday," suggested Molly, "then you'd use it only once a week, you know."

"Oh, what a funny verse this is," said Marjorie, as she read:

"I'm nothing to eat, I'm nothing to wear; You can only use me high up in the air."

"I know what it is," said Stella, with her funny little air of decision; "it's a kite! You could only use that high in the air, you know; and it's that Japanese sort that squeezes all up to nothing and then spreads out when you open it."

"I believe it is," said Midge, "only you know it said it was made of metal. But just listen to this next verse!

"I am not pretty, I am not gay, But you'll enjoy me every day."

The boxes were getting very small now, and Marjorie felt sure that the one she held in her hand must be the last one, unless, indeed, the gift was a cherry stone. The verse read:

"At last, Dear Mopsy, you've come to me! Behold your birthday gift! only a—"

As Marjorie read the last words she opened the box, and when she saw the contents she finished the rhyme herself by exclaiming, "key!"

CHAPTER XIV
"BREEZY INN"

Sure enough, the tiny box contained a small key tied with a bit of blue ribbon. Marjorie looked at it in bewilderment.

"It must unlock something!" cried Molly.

"Molly Moss," exclaimed Uncle Steve, "you have a wonderfully clever head for your years! How did you ever guess that a key would unlock something? You must have seen keys before!"

"But she never saw this one," cried Midge. "Oh, Uncle Steve, what is it for?"

"You've been in suspense quite long enough, and now we'll try to find a lock for that key to fit. Grandma and I will go first, and if you three young ladies will follow us, we will go and hunt for a keyhole."

Full of delightful anticipation, the three girls followed their older leaders. Marjorie was in the middle, her arms twined about Molly and Stella on either side, and their arms around her. Molly and Midge wanted to skip, but Stella never skipped, so the result was a somewhat joggly gait as they went down the path to the orchard.

The south meadow was a wide expanse of humpy grass-land, with only a few trees here and there.

Especially fine trees were two that were usually called the twin maples. These two very old trees grew side by side, their great trunks not more than four feet apart and their branches so intermingled that they were practically one tree in two parts. The delightful shade of this double tree afforded a favorite playground for the children, and they had missed it during the past week when they were forbidden to go into the meadow.

As they neared the meadow, Marjorie grew more and more amazed. There was nothing unusual in sight: no swing, no merry-go-round, and certainly nothing that a key could unlock. They reached the twin maples, and then Uncle Steve said: "If you'll all step around to the other side of this tree I think we may discover that missing keyhole."

The girls scampered around, and, looking up into the tree, they saw such an astonishing sight that the three simply sat down on the ground and stared at it. It was nothing more nor less than a house, a real little house high above the ground and nestled into the branches of the trees, just as a bird's nest might be.

The house, which was big enough for the girls to have gone into if they could have reached it, had a front door and a window on either side. There was a veranda on which stood three small rustic benches, quite strong enough to have held the three girls had they had wings to fly up there. The veranda had a railing around it, above which hung two hanging-baskets filled with bright flowers.

The door was shut and a keyhole could be distinctly seen.

"There's the keyhole, Mopsy, which I have reason to think will fit your key," said Uncle Steve.

"But I can't reach up to it," said Marjorie, looking very puzzled.
"What's the house for? Is it for birds?"
"Yes, for three birds that I know of, who wear gingham dresses and hair ribbons."

"But we don't wear wings," interrupted Marjorie. "Oh, Uncle Steve, do tell me what that house is for!"

"It's for you, chickabiddy, and if you'd like to go up there I'll show you a way."

Uncle Steve stepped over to the double trunk, and reaching up pulled down something, which proved to be a weight hung on the end of a long cord. The cord reached up to the veranda of the little house.

"Here," said Uncle Steve, as he put the weight into Marjorie's hand, "this is perhaps as useful a birthday gift as the key I gave you. Pull hard, and see what happens."

Marjorie pulled hard, and as she pulled, a rope ladder came tumbling down from the edge of the little porch. It was a queer-looking ladder, the sides being of rope and the rounds of wood, while the top seemed to be securely fastened to the veranda floor.

"There you are," said Uncle Steve; "there's your birthday gift, and all you have to do is to skip up there, unlock the door, and take possession."

But instead of doing this, Marjorie, with a squeal of delight, threw her arms around Uncle Steve's neck.

"You dear, old, blessed uncle!" she cried. "I understand it all now; but truly I couldn't think how we were ever going to get up there. It's a lovely surprise, the best I ever had! You are SO good to me, and Grandma, too!"

Having nearly squeezed the breath out of Uncle Steve, Marjorie left him, and flying over to Grandma, treated her to a similar demonstration. And then, with her precious key tightly clasped in her hand, she started to climb the rather wabbly ladder. Impetuous Molly was crazy to follow, but Uncle Steve declared that it was the law of the house that there must never be more than one on the ladder at a time.

Though Marjorie became accustomed to it afterward, it was not an easy matter to climb the rope ladder for the first time; but under Uncle Steve's direction she began to learn the trick of it, and safely reached the top. Agile Molly scrambled up as if she had been used to rope ladders all her life; but to timid Stella the climbing seemed an impossible feat. But Uncle Steve held the ladder firmly at the bottom, and Marjorie encouraged her from the top, while Molly threw herself flat on the porch and reached down a helping hand.

At last the three girls were safely on the little veranda, and the sensation was as delightful as it was strange. To sit on the little benches, high above the ground, and look out straight across the meadow; and then, turning to either side, to see the great limbs and branches of the old maple-trees, was indeed a fairy-tale experience.

Over the door swung a quaint little old-fashioned signboard, on which in gilt letters were the words "Breezy Inn."

With bewildering anticipations of further delight, Marjorie took her little key and unlocked the door.

Grandma and Uncle Steve, watching from below, heard shouts of joy as the girls disappeared through the doorway.

But in a moment they reappeared at the windows, and their beaming faces told the tale of their happiness.

"Good-by," called Uncle Steve, "the presentation is over and 'Breezy Inn' is yours. I've fastened the ladder firmly, so you can go up and down as you choose. The furnishings are your birthday present from Grandma, but we're going back now to a house that we can get into; and you children had better show up there about dinner-time. Meanwhile, have all the fun you can."

Grandma and Uncle Steve went away, leaving the children to explore and make acquaintance of "Breezy Inn."

It was a fairy house, indeed; and yet, though tiny, everything seemed to be just large enough.

The interior of the house was one large room; and a smaller room, like an ell, at the back. The large room contained the front door and two front windows, also a window at each end. The smaller room had no outer exit, but three windows gave ample light and air.

The front room, or living-room, as Marjorie termed it, was pleasantly furnished. On the floor was a rug of grass-matting and the furniture was of light wicker. The sofa, chairs, and tables were not of a size for grown people, but were just right for twelve-year-old little girls. At one end were a few built-in bookshelves; at the other a wardrobe or cupboard, most convenient to keep things in.

Grandma's handiwork was shown in some dear little sofa-pillows and chair-cushions, in dainty, draped curtains and table covers.

The room at the back, Marjorie declared was a workroom. In the middle was a large table, just splendid to work at when making paper-dolls' houses or anything like that; and round the room were shelves and cupboards to hold materials.

"It just takes my breath away!" said Marjorie, as she sank down on the settee in the living-room; "I never saw anything like it! Can't we have just the best fun here all summer!"

"I should say we could!" declared Molly. "It seems almost as if it must be our birthdays too. We'll have just as much fun here as you will, Midge."

"Why, I couldn't have any fun at all without you two; at least, it would be very lonesome fun."

"I don't see how they ever built it," said Molly, who, by way of finding out, was hanging out of a window as far as she could and investigating the building.

"I know," said the wise Stella; "I read about one once; they nail the beams and things to the trunks of the trees and then they nail boards across, and then they build the house. But the one I read about wasn't as nice as this."

"I don't think there could be one as nice as this," declared Marjorie; "and we can fix it up a lot yet, you know. I shall bring some things down from my room, some of my favorite books for the book-shelves, and things like that."

"Do you suppose it will rain in, ever?" asked the practical Stella.

"No, of course not," said Molly, who was still examining the carpenter work. "See, these windows slide shut sideways, and then if you shut the door tight the rain couldn't get in, unless the roof leaks."

"Of course it doesn't!" declared Midget; "Uncle Steve wouldn't build me a house with a leaky roof. Did you ever see such cunning window curtains! Of course we don't need blinds, for the tree keeps the sun out. It does seem so queer to look out of the window and see only a tree."

"Look out of the front door," said Molly, "and you won't see a tree then. You'll just see grass and sky and cows. But what's this thing at the back, Mopsy? It looks like a pair of well-buckets."

"I don't know. What can it be?" said Mopsy, running to look.

There was a queer contraption that seemed to be something like a windlass and something like a dumbwaiter. It was at the very end of the veranda around the corner of the house.

"I know," said Stella quietly; "it's a kind of an elevator thing to pull up things when you want to."

71

"Why, so it is!" cried Marjorie. "This is the way it works." And releasing a big wooden button, she let the whole affair slide to the ground, and, then, grasping the handle of a crank, she began to draw it up again.

"Well, if that isn't great!" cried Molly. "We can boost up all sorts of things!"

"Here's something to boost up now," said Marjorie, who had spied Jane coming across the fields, with what was undoubtedly a tray of refreshment.

And sure enough, Grandma had sent some ginger-snaps and lemonade to furnish the first feast at "Breezy Inn."

"Your grandma wouldn't send much," explained Jane, "for she says you must all come back to the house at one o'clock for the birthday dinner, and it's well after eleven now. She sent your clock, Miss Midget, so you'll know when to come."

Apparently Jane knew more about the ways and means of "Breezy Inn" than the children did; for she directed them explicitly how to let down the dumbwaiter, and, then, after having carefully placed on it the tray of good things and the clock, she advised them about drawing it up. It worked almost like a well-bucket and was quite easy to manage. The tray reached the top in safety, and, in great glee, the girls arranged the little feast on the table in the living-room, and sat down to play tea-party.

"Isn't this lovely!" exclaimed Molly, as she took her seventh ginger-snap from the plate. "I don't see how your grandma knew that we were beginning to get hungry."

"Grandma always seems to know everything that's nice," said Marjorie. "Some day, girls, let's come out here and spend the whole day. We'll bring a lot of lunch, you know, and it will be just as if we lived here."

"Goody!" said Molly. "That will be heaps of fun. We'll all bring things; I know Mother will give me a pie."

"I'll like it," said Stella, with an expression of great satisfaction; "because up here you girls can't romp around so and run as you do down on the ground. When we come for a whole day let's bring a book of fairy stories and take turns reading aloud."

"All right," said Midge; "let's have it for a sort of a club, and meet here one day every week."

"Clubs ought to do something," observed Molly. "Charity, you know, or something like that."

"All right," said Midge; "let's make things and then sell them and get some money for the Dunns."

"What could we do?" asked Molly. "We couldn't have another bazaar, and, besides, I think the Dunns have enough money for the present."

"Don't let's work," said Stella, who was not very enterprising; "at least, not when we're up here. Let's just read or play paper dolls. If you want to work and make things, do them at home."

"I feel that way, too," said Midget; "let's just keep this for a playhouse. But maybe it isn't right; maybe we ought to do things for charity."

"Ask your grandma," said Molly; "she'll know what's right. But I expect they gave you this house to have fun in."

"I think they did, too," said Marjorie; "and, anyway, Molly, we could do both. We had lots of fun getting ready for the bazaar, and we did the charity besides."

"Well, let's read part of the time, anyway," said Stella; "I do love to read or to be read to."

"We will," agreed Marjorie, amiably, and Molly agreed, too.

CHAPTER XV
THE BROKEN LADDER

As the days went on, "Breezy Inn" became more and more a delight to the children. They never grew tired of it, but, on the contrary, new attractions connected with it were forever developing. Many additions had been made to the furnishings, each of the three girls having brought over treasures from her own store.

They had reading days, and paper-doll days, and game-playing days, and feast days, and days when they did nothing but sit on the little veranda and make plans. Often their plans were not carried out, and often they were, but nobody cared much which way it happened. Sometimes Stella sat alone on the little porch, reading. This would usually be when Molly and Midge were climbing high up into the branches of the old maple-trees. It was very delightful to be able to step off of one's own veranda onto the branch of a tree and then climb on up and up toward the blue sky. And especially, there being two girls to climb, it was very useful to have two trees.

But not every day did the girls spend in "Breezy Inn." Sometimes they roamed in the woods, or went rowing on the river, and sometimes they visited at each other's houses.

One pleasant afternoon in late July, Marjorie asked Grandma if she mightn't go to spend the afternoon at Stella's.

Mrs. Sherwood liked to have her go to Stella's, as the influence of the quiet little girl helped to subdue Marjorie's more excitable disposition, and about three o'clock Marjorie started off.

Grandma Sherwood looked after the child, as she walked away, with admiring eyes. Marjorie wore a dainty frock of white dimity, scattered with tiny pink flowers. A pink sash and hair-ribbons were fresh and crisply tied, and she carried the pretty parasol Stella had given her on her birthday.

With Marjorie, to be freshly dressed always made her walk decorously, and Grandma smiled as she saw the little girl pick her way daintily down the walk to the front gate, and along the road to Stella's, which, though only next door, was several hundred yards away.

As Marjorie passed out of sight, Grandma sighed a little to think how quickly the summer was flying by, for she dearly loved to have her grandchildren with her, and though, perhaps, not to be called favorite, yet Marjorie was the oldest and possessed a very big share of her grandmother's affection.

Soon after she reached Stella's, Molly came flying over. Molly, too, had on a clean afternoon dress, but that never endowed her with a sense of decorum, as it did Marjorie.

"Hello, girls," she cried, as she climbed over the veranda-railing and plumped herself down in the hammock. "What are we going to do this afternoon?"

"Let's read," said Stella, promptly.

"Read, read, read!" said Molly. "I'm tired of your everlasting reading.
Let's play tennis."
"It's too hot for tennis," said Stella, "and, besides, you girls haven't tennis shoes on and you'd spoil your shoes and the court, too."

"Oh, what do you think," said Mopsy, suddenly; "I have the loveliest idea! Only we can't do it this afternoon, because we're all too much dressed up. But I'll tell you about it, and we can begin to-morrow morning."

"What's your idea?" said Molly, rousing herself in the hammock and sitting with her chin in both hands as she listened.

"Why, I read it in the paper," said Marjorie, "and it's this. And it's a lovely way to make money; we could make quite a lot for the Dunns. It will be some trouble, but it would be a lot of fun, too."

"Yes, but what is it," said Stella, in her quietly patient way.

"You go out into the field," began Marjorie, "and you gather heaps and heaps of pennyroyal,—you take baskets, you know, and gather just pecks of it. Then you take it home and you put it in pails or tubs or anything with a lot of water. And then you leave it about two days, and then you drain it off, and then it's pennyroyal extract."

Marjorie announced the last words with a triumphant air, but her hearers did not seem very much impressed.

"What then?" asked Molly, evidently awaiting something more startling.

"Why, then, you put it in bottles, and paste labels on, and take it all around and sell it to people. They love to have it, you know, for mosquitoes or burns or something, and they pay you quite a lot, and then you have the money for charity."

The artistic possibilities began to dawn upon Stella.

"Yes," she said, "and I could make lovely labels, with fancy letters; and you and Molly could paste them on, and we could tie the corks in with little blue ribbons, like perfumery bottles."

"And we'll each bring bottles," cried Molly, becoming interested; "we have lots at our house. Let's start out now to gather the pennyroyal. We're not so awfully dressed up. This frock will wash, anyway."

"So will mine," said Marjorie, but she spoke with hesitation. She knew that Grandma would not like to have her wear that dainty fresh frock out into the fields.

But, for some reason, Stella, too, was inclined to go, and with the trio, two against one always carried the day; and linking arms, in half a minute the three were skipping away toward the field. They had not asked permission, because the fields were part of Mr. Martin's property, and Stella was practically on her own home ground, though at a good distance from the house.

Enthusiastic over their new plan, the girls worked with a will, and, having carelessly gone off without any basket, they found themselves obliged to hold up the skirts of their dresses to carry their harvest.

"I should think we had enough to sell to everybody in Morristown," declared Molly, as, tired and flushed, she surveyed the great heap she had piled into her dress skirt.

"So should I," agreed Midget, gathering up more and more of her pretty dimity, now, alas! rumpled and stained almost beyond recognition.

Stella had a good share, though not so much as the others, and she stood calmly inquiring what they were going to do with it.

"There's no use taking it to my house," she declared, "for mother would only tell me to throw it away,—I know she would."

"Wouldn't she let us make the extract?" asked Marjorie.

"She wouldn't care how much we made it, but she wouldn't let me make it at home, I know, because she hates a mess."

"I don't believe Grandma would like it either," said Marjorie, with a sudden conviction; "it is awful messy, and it smells pretty strong. But I'll tell you what, girls: let's take it all right to 'Breezy Inn.' Then we can put it to soak right away. We can get water from the brook, and there are plenty of pails and things there to make the extract in."

"We can call it The Breezy Extract," said Stella; "that'll look pretty painted on the labels."

"Breezy Extract is silly," said Molly; "Breezy-Inn Extract is prettier."

"All right," said Stella, good-naturedly. "Come on, I'm in a hurry to begin. I'll paint the labels, while you girls make the stuff."

So they trudged across the field to Breezy Inn, dumped their heaps of pennyroyal into the dumb-waiter, and themselves scrambled gayly up the rope ladder.

Almost before Molly and Midge had pulled up their somewhat odorous burden, Stella had seated herself at the table to work at the labels. The child was devoted to work of this sort, and was soon absorbed in designing artistic letters to adorn the bottles.

Midge and Molly worked away with a will. Unheeding their pretty summer frocks, and, indeed, there was little use now for care in that direction, they brought water from the brook, hauled it up the dumbwaiter, and filled several good-sized receptacles with steeping pennyroyal flowers.

Their work finished, they were anxious to start for home at once and begin a search for the bottles, but Stella begged them to stay a little longer until she should have finished the design she was making.

So Midge and Molly wandered out on the veranda, and amused themselves by jerking the rope ladder up and down. By a clever mechanical contrivance the ladder went up and down something on the principle of an automatic shade roller. It was great fun to roll it up and feel a certain security in the thought that nobody could get into "Breezy Inn" unless they saw fit to let down the ladder. Not that anybody ever wanted to, but it was fun to think so, and, moreover, the rolling ladder was most useful in the playing of certain games, where an unlucky princess was imprisoned in a castle tower.

But somehow, as they were idly jerking the ladder up and down, an accident happened. Something snapped at the top, and with a little cracking sound, the whole ladder broke loose from its fastenings and fell to the ground.

"Oh, Midget!" cried Molly, aghast, "whatever shall we do now? We can't get down, and we'll have to stay here until somebody happens to come by this way."

"That may not be for several days," said Midget, cheerfully. "Carter never hardly comes down into this meadow. Pooh, Molly, we can get down some way."

"Yes; but how?" insisted Molly, who realized the situation more truly than Marjorie.

"Oh, I don't know," responded Midge, carelessly. "We might go down in the dumb-waiter."

"No; your uncle said, positively, we must never go down on that. It isn't strong enough to hold even one of us at a time."

"I guess I could jump."

"I guess you couldn't! You'd sprain your ankles and break your collar bones."

"Oh, pshaw, Molly, there must be some way down. Let's ask Stella. She can always think of something."

"No; don't tell Stella. She can't think of any way, and it would scare her to pieces. I tell you, Mops, there ISN'T any way down. It's too high to jump and we can't climb. We could climb UP the tree, but not DOWN."

At last Marjorie began to realize that they were in a difficulty. She looked all around the house, and there really was no way by which the girls could get down. They went into the living-room, where Stella sat at the table, drawing.

"I'm ready to go home," she said, looking up as they entered. "This is finished, and, anyway, it's getting so dark I can't see any more."

"Dark!" exclaimed Marjorie. "Why, it isn't five o'clock yet."

"I don't care what time it is," said Stella; "it's getting awfully dark, just the same."

And sure enough it was, and a few glances at the sky showed the reason. What was undoubtedly a severe thunderstorm was rapidly approaching, and dark masses of cloud began to roll over each other and pile up higher and higher toward the zenith.

"It's a thunder shower, that's what it is," declared Stella; "let's scramble down the ladder quick, and run for home. Let's all run to your house, Marjorie, it's nearer."

Midge and Molly looked at each other.

There was no help for it, so Marjorie said: "We can't go down the ladder, Stella, because it's broken down."

"What! Who broke it?"

"We did," said Molly; "that is, we were playing with it and somehow it broke itself. Of course, we didn't do it on purpose."

Stella's face turned white. "How shall we get down?" she said.

"We CAN'T get down," said Midge, cheerfully; "we'll have to stay up. But the roof doesn't leak; I asked Uncle, and he said it was perfectly watertight."

"But I don't want to stay up here in a storm," said Stella, and her lips began to quiver.

"Now, don't you cry, Stella!" said Molly, who, if truth be told, was on the verge of tears herself.

Meantime, the darkness was rapidly increasing. It was one of those sudden showers where a black pall of cloud seems to envelop the whole universe, and the very air takes on a chill that strikes a terror of its own, even to a stout heart.

The three little girls sat looking at each other in despair.

Each was very much frightened, but each was trying to be brave. It had all happened so suddenly that they had even yet scarcely realized that they were in real danger, when suddenly a terrible clap of thunder burst directly above their heads, accompanied by a blinding flash of lightning.

Stella screamed and then burst into wild crying; Molly turned white and gritted her teeth in a determination not to cry; while Marjorie, with big tears rolling down her cheeks, put her arms around Stella in a vain endeavor to comfort her.

Molly crept up to the other two, and intertwining their arms, the three huddled together, shivering with fear and dismay.

One after another, the terrible thunderbolts crashed and rolled, and the fearful lightning glared at intervals.

Then, with a swish and a splash, the rain began. It came down in gusty torrents, and dashed in at the open windows like a spray.

Molly and Marjorie jumped up and flew to shut the windows, but Stella remained crouched in a pathetic little heap.

"Somebody will come to get us," whispered Molly, trying to be hopeful and to cheer the others.

"No, they won't," said Marjorie, despairingly; "for Grandma thinks I'm over at Stella's, and your mother thinks you're there, too."

"Yes, but Stella's mother will hunt us up; somebody is SURE to come," persisted Molly.

"No, she won't," said a weak little voice; "for I told Mother that we might stay home this afternoon, and we might go over to Molly's. And she'll think we're over there."

"It wouldn't matter if the ladder WAS up," said Molly, "for we couldn't go out in this pouring rain, and we might get struck by lightning, too."

"Under a tree is the very worst place to be in a thunderstorm," said Stella, lifting her white, little face, and staring at the girls with big, scared eyes.

Just then another terrible crash and flash made them all grasp each other again, and then, without further restraint, they all cried together.

The storm increased. The winds simply raged, and though the old maple-trees were too sturdy to shake much, yet the little house swayed some, and all about could be heard the cracking and snapping of branches.

"I think—" began Molly, but even as she spoke there came the loudest crash of all. It was the splitting of the heavens, and with it came a fierce, sudden flash of flame that blinded them all.

The girls fell apart from one another through the mere shock, and when Molly and Midge dazedly opened their eyes, they saw Stella crumpled in a little heap on the floor.

CHAPTER XVI
FIRECRACKERS
"Is she dead?" screamed Molly. "Oh, Marjorie, is she dead?"

"I don't know," said Marjorie, whose face was almost as white as
Stella's, as she leaned over the unconscious little girl.
Although they tried, they couldn't quite manage to lift Stella up on the couch, so Marjorie sat down on the floor and took the poor child's head on her knee, while Molly ran for water.

"I'm sure it's right to douse people with water when they faint," said Molly, as she sprinkled Stella's face liberally; "and she is only in a faint, isn't she, Marjorie? Because if people are really struck by lightning they burn up, don't they, Marjorie?"

While she talked, Molly was excitedly pouring water promiscuously over
Stella, until the child looked as if she had been out in the storm.
Marjorie was patting Stella's cheek and rubbing her hands, but it all seemed of no avail; and, though Stella was breathing softly, they could not restore her to consciousness.

"It's dreadful," said Marjorie, turning to Molly with a look of utter despair, "and we MUST do something! It isn't RIGHT for us two little girls to try to take care of Stella. We MUST get Grandma here, somehow."

"But how CAN we?" said Molly. "The ladder is down, you know, and we can't possibly get down from the house. I'd try to jump, but it's fifteen feet, and I'd be sure to break some bones, and we'd be worse off than ever."

The two girls were too frightened to cry; they were simply appalled by the awful situation and at their wits' end to know what to do.

"It was bad enough," wailed Marjorie, "when we were all wide awake and could be frightened together; but with Stella asleep, or whatever she is, it's perfectly horrible."

"She isn't asleep," said Molly, scrutinizing the pale little face, "but she's stunned with the shock, and I'm sure I don't know what to do. We ought to have smelling-salts, or something, to bring her to."

"We ought to have somebody that knows something to look after her.

Molly, we MUST get Grandma here. I believe I'll try to jump myself, but I suppose I'd just sprain my ankle and lie there in the storm till I was all washed away. What CAN we do?"

"We could holler, but nobody could hear us, it's raining so hard. The thunder and lightning aren't so bad now, but the rain and wind are fearful."

Molly was flying about the room, peeping out at one window after another, and then flying back to look at Stella, who still lay unconscious.

"If we only had a megaphone," said Marjorie, "though I don't believe we could scream loud enough through that even, to make Carter hear. What do people do when they're shipwrecked?"

"They send up rockets," said Molly, wisely.

"We haven't any rockets; but, oh, Molly! we have some firecrackers. They've been here ever since Fourth of July; those big cannon crackers, you know! Do you suppose we could fire off some of those, and Carter would hear them?"

"The very thing! But how can we fire them in this awful rain? It would put them right out."

"We MUST do it! It's our only chance!"

Carefully putting a pillow under Stella's head, they left her lying on the floor, while they ran for the firecrackers.

Sure enough they were big ones, and there were plenty of them. It would be difficult to fire them in the rain, but, as Marjorie said, it MUST be done. Keeping them carefully in a covered box, the girls went out on the little veranda, closing the door behind them. A wooden box, turned up on its side, formed sufficient protection from the rain to get a cracker lighted, and Marjorie bravely held it until it was almost ready to explode, and then flung it out into the storm. It went off, but to the anxious girls the noise seemed muffled by the rain.

They tried another and another, but with little hope that Carter would hear them.

"Let's put them all in a tin pan," said Marjorie, "and put the box on top of them to keep them dry, and then set them all off at once."

"All right," said Molly, "but I'm afraid Carter will think it's thunder."

However, it seemed the best plan, and after lighting the end of the twisted string, the girls ran into the house and shut the door.

Such a racket as followed! The crackers went off all at once. The box flew off, and the tin pan tumbled down, and the little veranda was a sight to behold!

It sounded like Fourth of July, but to the two girls, watching from the window, there was no effect of celebration.

80

But their desperate plan succeeded. Carter heard the racket, and did not mistake it for thunder; but, strangely enough, realized at once what it was.

"It's them crazy children in their tree-house," he exclaimed; "but what the mischief do they be settin' off firecrackers for, in the pouring rain? Howsomever I'll just go and see what's up, for like as not they've burned their fingers, if so be that they haven't put their eyes out."

As Carter started from the greenhouse, where he had been working, the torrents of rain that beat in his face almost made him change his mind, but he felt a sense of uneasiness about Marjorie, and something prompted him to go on. In a stout raincoat, and under a big umbrella, he made his way across the field through the storm toward "Breezy Inn."

"My land!" he exclaimed, "if that ladder ain't disappeared. What will them youngsters be up to next?"

But even as he noticed the broken ladder, the door flew open, and Marjorie and Molly popped their heads out.
"Oh, Carter!" Marjorie screamed; "do get a ladder, and hurry up! Ours is broken down, and Stella is struck by lightning, and, oh, Carter, do help us!"

Carter took in the situation at a glance. He said nothing, for it was no time for words. He saw the broken ladder could not be repaired in a minute; and, turning, he ran swiftly back to the barn for another ladder. A long one was necessary, and with Moses to help him they hurried the ladder across the field and raised it.

Another fortunate effect of the firecracker explosion had been to rouse Stella. Partly owing to the noise of the explosion, and partly because the effect of the shock was wearing away, Stella had opened her eyes and, realizing what had happened, promptly made up for lost time by beginning to cry violently. Also, the reaction at finding Stella herself again, and the relief caused by the appearance of Carter, made Molly and Marjorie also break down, and when Carter came bounding up the ladder he found three girls, soaking wet as to raiment, and diligently adding to the general dampness by fast-flowing tears.

"What is it, now?" he inquired, and if his tone sounded impatient, it was scarcely to be wondered at. For the battle-scarred veranda and the drenched condition of the room, together with a broken ladder, surely betokened mischief of some sort.

"Oh, Carter," cried Marjorie, "never mind us, but can't you take Stella to the house somehow? She was struck by lightning, and she's been dead for hours! She only just waked up when she heard the firecrackers! Did you hear them, Carter?"

"Did I hear them! I did that—not being deaf. Faith, I thought it was the last trump! You're a caution, Miss Midget!" But even as Carter spoke he began to realize that the situation was more serious than a mere childish scrape. He had picked up little Stella, who was very limp and white, and who was still sobbing hysterically.

"Struck by lightning, is it? There, there, little girl, never mind now,

I'll take care of ye."

Holding Stella gently in his arms, Carter looked out of the window and considered.

"I could take her down the ladder, Miss Midget, but it's raining so hard she'd be drenched before we could reach the house. Not that she could be much wetter than she is. Was she out in the rain?"

"No, that's where we threw water on her to make her unfaint herself. Can't we all go home, Carter? Truly we can't get any wetter, and we'll all catch cold if we don't."

"That's true," agreed Carter, as he deliberated what was best to do.

Though not a large man, Carter seemed to fill the little room with his grown-up presence, and the children were glad to shift their responsibility on to him.

"The thunder is melting away," he said at last, "and the lightning is nothin' to speak of; and a drop more of wet won't hurt you, so I think I'd better take ye all to your grandma's as soon as possible. I'll carry little Miss Stella, and do ye other two climb down the ladder mighty careful and don't add no broken necks to your distresses."

So down the ladder, which Moses on the ground was holding firmly, Carter carried Stella, who, though fully conscious, was nervous and shaken, and clung tightly around Carter's neck.

Midge and Molly followed, and then the procession struck out across the field for home.

"I s'pose," whispered Midget to Molly, "it's perfectly awful; but now that Stella's all right, I can't help thinking this is sort of fun, to be walking out in the storm, without any umbrella, and soaking wet from head to foot!"

Molly squeezed her friend's hand. "I think so, too," she whispered. "The thunder and lightning were terrible, and I was almost scared to death; but now that everything's all right, I can't help feeling gay and glad!"

And so these two reprehensible young madcaps smiled at each other, and trudged merrily along across soaking fields, in a drenching rain, and rescued from what had been a very real danger indeed.

During all this, Grandma Sherwood had been sitting placidly in her room, assuming that Marjorie was safely under shelter next door. Molly's mother had, of course, thought the same, and Stella's mother, finding the girls nowhere about, had concluded they were either at Molly's or Marjorie's.

Owing to the condition of the party he was bringing, Carter deemed it best to make an entrance by the kitchen door.

"There!" he said, as he landed the dripping Stella on a wooden chair, "for mercy's sake, Eliza, get the little lady into dry clothes as quick as you can!"

"The saints presarve us!" exclaimed Eliza, for before she had time to realize Stella's presence, Midge and Molly bounded in, scattering spray all over the kitchen and dripping little pools of water from their wet dresses.

Stella had ceased crying, but looked weak and ill. The other two, on the contrary, were capering about, unable to repress their enjoyment of this novel game.

Hearing the commotion, Grandma Sherwood came to the kitchen, and not unnaturally supposed it all the result of some new prank.

"What HAVE you been doing?" she exclaimed. "Why didn't you stay at
Stella's and not try to come home through this rain?"
Marjorie, drenched as she was, threw herself into her grandmother's arms.

"Oh, if you only knew!" she cried; "you came near not having your bad little Mopsy any more! And Stella's mother came nearer yet! Why, Grandma, we were in the tree-house, and it was struck by lightning, and Stella was killed, at least for a little while, and the ladder broke down, and we couldn't get down ourselves, and so we sent off rockets of distress, I mean firecrackers, and then Carter came and rescued us all!"

As Marjorie went on with her narrative, Grandma Sherwood began to understand that the children had been in real danger, and she clasped her little grandchild closer until her own dress was nearly as wet as the rest of them.

"And so you see, Grandma," she proceeded, somewhat triumphantly, "it wasn't mischief a bit! It was a—an accident that might have happened to anybody; and, oh, Grandma dear, wasn't it a narrow squeak for Stella!"

"Howly saints!" ejaculated Eliza; "to think of them dear childer bein' shtruck be thunder, an' mighty near killed! Och, but ye're the chrazy wans! Whyever did ye go to yer tree-top shanty in such a shtorm? Bad luck to the botherin' little house!"

"Of course it didn't rain when we went there," said Marjorie, who was now dancing around Eliza, and flirting her wet ruffles at her, in an endeavor to tease the good-natured cook.

But even as they talked, Mrs. Sherwood and Eliza were taking precautions against ill effects of the storm.

Mrs. Sherwood devoted her attention to Stella, as the one needing it most, while Eliza looked after the other two.

The three children were treated to a hot bath and vigorous rubbings, and dry clothes, and in a short time, attired in various kimonos and dressing-gowns from Marjorie's wardrobe, the three victims sat in front of the kitchen range, drinking hot lemonade and eating ginger cookies.

As Marjorie had said, there had been no wrongdoing; not even a mischievous prank, except, perhaps, the breaking down of the ladder, and yet it seemed a pity that Stella should have suffered the most, when she never would have dreamed of staying at the tree-house after it began to look like rain, had it not been for the others.

However, there was certainly no scolding or punishment merited by any one; and Grandma Sherwood was truly thankful that the three were safe under her roof.

After the storm had entirely cleared away, Carter carried Stella home, and Mrs. Sherwood went with them to explain matters. Molly went skipping home, rather pleased than otherwise, to have such an exciting adventure to relate to her mother.

When Uncle Steve came home he was greatly interested in Midget's tale of the tragedy, and greatly pleased that small heroine of the occasion by complimenting her on her ingenuity in using the firecrackers. The breaking of the ladder, he declared, was an accident, and said a new and stronger one should be put up. Furthermore, he decreed that a telephone connection should be established between "Breezy Inn" and Grandma's house, so that victims of any disaster could more easily summon aid.

"That will be lovely," said Marjorie, "but they say telephones are dangerous in thunderstorms; so, perhaps, it's just as well that we didn't have one there to-day."

CHAPTER XVII
PENNYROYAL

It was several days before the children went to "Breezy Inn" again, but one pleasant sunshiny morning found them climbing the new ladder as gayly as if no unpleasant experience were connected with its memory.

Carter had cleaned up the veranda, though powder marks still showed in some places.

"Why, girls," exclaimed Marjorie, "here's our pennyroyal extract! I had forgotten every single thing about it. The high old time we had that day swept it all out of my head."

"I remembered it," said Molly, "but I thought it had to extract itself for a week."

"No, four days is enough. It must be done now; it smells so, anyway."

The girls all sniffed at the pails of spicy-smelling water, and, after wisely dipping their fingers in it and sniffing at them, they concluded it was done.

"It's beautiful," said Marjorie; "I think it's a specially fine extract, and we'll have no trouble in selling heaps of it. Don't let's tell anybody until we've made a whole lot of money; and then we'll tell Grandma it's for the Dunns, and she'll be so surprised to think we could do it."

"Where are the bottles?" asked Stella. "I can finish up the labels, while you girls are filling the bottles and tying the corks in."

"Let's tie kid over the top," suggested Molly, "like perfume bottles, you know. You just take the wrists of old kid gloves and tie them on with a little ribbon, and then snip the edges all around like they snip the edges of a pie."

"Lovely!" cried Midget, "and now I'll tell you what: let's all go home and get a lot of bottles and corks and old kid gloves and ribbons and everything, and then come back here and fix the bottles up right now."

"You two go," said Stella, who was already absorbed in the work of making labels; "that will give me time to do these things. They're going to be awfully pretty."

So Midge and Molly scampered off to their homes, and rummaged about for the materials they wanted.

They had no trouble in finding them, for the elder people in both houses were accustomed to odd demands from the children, and in less than half an hour the girls were back again, each with a basket full of bottles, old gloves, and bits of ribbon.

"Did your mother ask you what you wanted them for?" said Mops to Molly.

"No; she just told me where they were, in a cupboard in the attic; and told me to get what I wanted and not bother her, because she was making jelly."

"I got mine from Eliza, so Grandma doesn't know anything about it; and now we can keep it secret, and have a lovely surprise."

What might have seemed work, had they been doing it for some one else, was play to the children then; and Midge and Molly carefully strained their precious extract from the leaves and bottled it and corked it with care. They tied neatly the bits of old gloves over the corks, though it was not an easy task, and when finished did not present quite the appearance of daintily-topped perfume bottles.

And Stella's labels, though really good work for a little girl of eleven, were rather amateurish. But the three business partners considered the labels admirable works of art, and pasted them on the bottles with undisguised pride. Though pennyroyal was spelled with one n, they didn't notice it, and the finished wares seemed to them a perfect result of skilled labor.

"Now," said Marjorie, as she sat with her chin in her hands, gazing proudly at the tableful of bottles, "it's dinner-time. Let's all go home, and then this afternoon, after we're dressed, let's come here and get the bottles, and each take a basketful, and go and sell them."

"We'll all go together, won't we?" asked Stella, whose shyness stood sadly in the way of her being a successful saleswoman.

"Yes, if you like," said Marjorie; "we'd get along faster by going separately; but it will be more fun to go together, so that's what we'll do."

About two o'clock, the three met again at "Breezy Inn." Each was freshly attired in a spick-and-span clean gingham, and they wore large shade hats.

"I thought Grandma would suspect something when I put my hat on," said Marjorie, "because I always race out here without any, but, by good luck, she didn't see me."

"Mother asked me where I was going," said Molly, "and I told her to 'Breezy Inn.' It almost seemed deceitful, but I think, as we're working for charity, it's all right. You know you mustn't let your left hand know what your right hand is up to."

"That isn't what that means," said Stella, who was a conscientious little girl; and, indeed, they all were, for though inclined to mischief, Midge and Molly never told stories, even by implication.

"But I think it's all right," went on Stella, earnestly, "because it's a surprise. You know Christmas or Valentine's day, it's all right to surprise people, even if you have to 'most nearly deceive them."

And so with no qualms of their honest little hearts, the three started off gayly to peddle their dainty wares for the cause of charity.

"Let's go straight down to the village," suggested Molly, "and let's stop at every house on the way,—there aren't very many,—and then when we get where the houses are thicker we can go separately if we want to."

"I don't want to," insisted Stella; "I'll stay with one of you, anyway."

"All right," said Midget, "and we'll take turns in doing the talking.
This is Mrs. Clarke's house; shall I talk here?"
"Yes," said Molly, "and I'll help you; and if Stella doesn't want to say anything, she needn't."

The three girls with their baskets skipped along the flower-bordered walk to Mrs. Clarke's front door and rang the bell. The white-capped maid, who answered the door, listened to their inquiries for Mrs. Clarke, looked curiously at the bottles, and then said: "Mrs. Clarke is not at home."

"Are you sure?" said Marjorie, in a despairing voice. It seemed dreadful to lose a sale because the lady chanced to be out.

"Yes," said the maid shortly, and closed the door in the very faces of the disappointed children.

Troubled, but not disheartened, the girls walked back along the path, a little less gayly, and trudged on to the next house.

Here the lady herself opened the door.

"Do you want to buy some pennyroyal extract?" began Marjorie, a little timidly, for the expression on the lady's face was not at all cordial.

86

"It's fine," broke in Molly, who saw that Midge needed her support; "it's lovely for mosquito bites, you just rub it on and they're all gone!"

The lady seemed to look a little interested, and Stella being honestly anxious to do her share, so far conquered her timidity as to say in a faint little voice, "We made it ourselves."

"Made it yourselves?" exclaimed the lady. "No, indeed, I don't want any!" And again the cruel door was closed upon the little saleswomen.

"It was my fault," wailed Stella, as they went away with a crestfallen air; "if I hadn't said we made it ourselves, she would have bought it. Oh, girls, let me go home and make labels. I don't like this selling, much."

Midge and Molly both felt sure that it was Stella's speech that had stopped the sale, but they were too polite to say so, and Midge answered:

"Never mind, Stella dear, I don't think she was very anxious for it, anyway, but, perhaps, at the next house you needn't say anything. You don't mind, do you?"

"Mind! No, indeed! I only said that to help along, and it didn't help."

So, at the next house, Stella was glad to stand demurely in the background, and this time Molly took her turn at introducing the subject.

A young lady was in a hammock on the veranda, and as they went up the steps she rose to greet them.

"What in the world have you there?" she said, gayly, flinging down the book she was reading and looking at the children with interest.

"Pennyroyal extract," said Molly, "perfectly fine for mosquito bites, bruises, cuts, scarlet fever, colds, coughs, or measles."

The young lady seemed to think it very amusing, and sitting down on the top step, began to laugh.

"It must be, indeed, handy to have in the house," she said; "where did you get it?"

The girls were dismayed. If they said they made it themselves, probably she wouldn't buy any. They looked at each other uncertainly, and said nothing.

"I hope you came by it honestly," went on the young lady, looking at them in surprise; "you couldn't have—of course, you didn't—"

"Of course we didn't steal it!" cried Molly, indignantly, "if that's what you mean. It's ours, our very own, every drop of it! But—we don't want to tell you where we got it."

"It sounds delightfully mysterious," said the young lady, still smiling very much, "and I don't really care where you did get it. Of course I want some, as it seems to be a very useful article, and I'm quite liable to attacks of—measles."

Marjorie looked up quickly to see if this very pretty young lady was not making fun of them, but she seemed to be very much in earnest, and, indeed, was already selecting a bottle from each of the three baskets.

"I'll take these three," she said; "how much are they?"

The girls looked at each other. Not once had it occurred to them to consider what price they were to ask, and what to say they did not know.

"Why," began Marjorie, "I should think—"

"Twenty-five cents apiece," said Molly, decidedly. She knew it was a large price, considering that the extract cost nothing, but she wanted to swell the charity funds.

"Well, that's very reasonable," said the young lady, who still seemed very much amused; "I will give you the money at once," and she took some change from a little gold purse which hung at her belt. "But if I may advise you," she went on, "you'd better raise your price. That's really too cheap for this most useful article."

The children were so astonished at this speech that they made no reply, except to thank the kind young lady, and bid her good-by.

"Now, THAT'S something like!" exclaimed Marjorie, as they reached the road again. "Wasn't she lovely? And to think, she said we ought to ask more money for the extract! This is a splendid business."

"Fine!" agreed Molly; "we'll sell off all this to-day, and to-morrow we'll make another lot and sell that. We'll get lots of money for the Dunns."

"We'll make more next time," said Midge, "and I'll get Carter to drive us round so we won't have to carry it; for we may sell two or three hundred bottles every day."

"But I can't make so many labels," said Stella, aghast at the outlook.

"Of course you can't," said Molly; "but I'll tell you what! We'll ask them to give the bottles back as soon as they've emptied them, and then we can use them over again, you know."

Midge was a little dubious about asking for the bottles back, but just then they turned into the next house.

It was Marjorie's turn to speak, and greatly encouraged by their late success, she began: "Would you like to buy some pennyroyal extract? For mosquitoes, burns, and bruises. It's only fifty cents a bottle, and we'll take the bottles back."

The lady, who had opened the door, looked at the children as if they were escaped lunatics.

"Don't come around here playing your tricks on me," she exclaimed; "I won't stand it. Take your bottles and be off!"

She did not shut the door upon them, but so irate was her expression that the girls were glad to go away.

"Wasn't she awful!" exclaimed Stella, with a troubled face. "Truly, girls, I don't like this. I'm going home."

"No, you're not, either!" said Marjorie. "Of course, it isn't all pleasant, but when you're working for charity, you mustn't mind that. And, besides, like as not the people at the next house will be lovely."

But they weren't; and one after another the people, to whom they offered their wares, refused even to look at them.

At last, when they were well-nigh discouraged, a kind lady, to whom they offered the extract, seemed a little more interested than the others.

"Why," she said, looking at Stella, "aren't you Guy Martin's little girl?"

"Yes'm," said Stella, meekly, wondering if this fact would interfere with the sale of the goods.

"Well, then, I must surely buy some," said the lady, smiling; "how much is it?"

"Fifty cents a bottle, if you give the bottle back," said Stella, who felt that the lady's friendliness toward her demanded that she should answer?

"Fifty cents a bottle!" exclaimed the lady. "Surely you can't mean that! Why, pennyroyal extract isn't worth a cent a quart!"

The girls looked genuinely disturbed. This was a different opinion, indeed, from that advanced by the pretty lady who had bought three bottles!

Marjorie suddenly began to feel as if she were doing something very foolish, and something which she ought not to have undertaken without Grandma's advice.

"Is that all it's worth, truly?" she asked, looking straightforwardly into the lady's eyes.

"Why, yes, my dear,—I'm sure it could not have a higher market value."

"Then we don't want to sell you any," said Marjorie, whose sense of honesty was aroused; and picking up her basket from the porch, she turned toward the street, walking fast, and holding her head high in the air, while her cheeks grew very red.

Molly followed her, uncertain as to what to do next, and Stella trailed along behind, a dejected little figure, indeed, with her heavy basket on her arm.

CHAPTER XVIII
WELCOME GIFTS

"It's all wrong!" declared Marjorie. "I didn't see it before, but I do now. That lady was right, and we oughtn't to try to sell anything that's worth less than a cent for fifty cents, or twenty-five either."

"Shall we go home?" asked Molly, who always submitted to Marjorie's decisions.

"I don't think it's wrong," began Stella. "Of course the pennyroyal isn't worth much, but we worked to get it, and to make it, and to fix it up and all; and, besides, people always pay more than things are worth when they're for charity."

Marjorie's opinion veered around again. The three were sitting on a large stepping-stone under some shady trees, and Marjorie was thinking out the matter to her own satisfaction before they should proceed.

"Stella, I believe you're right, after all," she said. "Now I'll tell you what we'll do: we'll go to one more place, and if it's a nice lady, we'll ask her what she thinks about it, for I'd like the advice of a grown-up."

This seemed a fair proposition, and the three wandered in at the very place where they had been sitting on the stone.

With renewed courage, they rang the door bell. It was Marjorie's turn to speak, and the words were on the tip of her tongue. Being somewhat excited, she began her speech as the door began to open.

"Don't you want to buy some pennyroyal extract?" she said rapidly; "it's perfectly fine for mosquitoes, measles, and burns, and scarlet fever! It isn't worth a cent a quart, but we sell it for fifty cents a bottle, if you give the bottles back. But if you don't think it's right for us to sell it, we won't."

Marjorie would not have been quite so mixed up in her speech but for the fact that after she was fairly started upon it, she raised her eyes to the person she was addressing, and instead of a kind and sweet-faced lady she beheld a very large, burly, and red-faced gentleman.

Not wishing to appear embarrassed, she floundered on with her speech, though in reality she hardly knew what she was saying.

"Well, upon my soul!" exclaimed the red-faced gentleman, in a loud, deep voice, "here's a pretty kettle of fish. Young ladies peddling extract at decent people's houses!" He glared at the girls with a ferocious expression, and then went on, in even louder tones: "What do you MEAN by such doings? Have you a license? Don't you know that people who sell goods without a license must be arrested? I've a notion to clap every one of you in jail!"

As might have been expected, Stella began to cry, while Midge and Molly gazed at the red-faced old man as if fascinated. They wanted to run away, but something in his look held them there; and, anyway, they couldn't go and leave Stella, who had dropped in a little heap on the floor of the piazza and hidden her face in her arms, while convulsive sobs shook her slender little frame.

At sight of Stella's tears, a sudden and wonderful change seemed to come over the old gentleman. His ferocious expression gave way to an anxious smile, and, stooping, he picked Stella up in his arms, saying: "There, there, baby! don't be frightened; that was only my joking. Why, bless your heart, I wasn't a mite in earnest. There, there, now, don't cry; I'll buy all your extract,—every single drop,—and pay any price you want; and I'll give you back all the bottles, and all the baskets, and all the extract, too, if you want it, and some lovely peaches into the bargain! There, brace up now, and forgive your old Uncle Bill for teasing you so! Jail, indeed! I'll take you into the house instead, and find some plum-cake for you!"

Carrying Stella in his big, strong arms, the strange old gentleman ushered Midge and Molly into the house and made straight for the dining-room.

"Folks all gone away," he went on, still in his gruff, deep tones, but somehow they now sounded very kind; "gone away for an all-day picnic, and left me alone to shift for myself. Jolly glad to have company—jolly glad to entertain you. Here's peaches, here's cake. Have a glass of milk?"

The old man bustled around and seemed so anxious to dispel the unpleasant impression he had made at first that Molly and Midge met him halfway, and beamed happily as they accepted the pleasant refreshments he set out.

"Fall to, fall to," he said, rubbing his big hands together, as he watched the children do justice to the feast.

The girls suddenly discovered that they were both tired and hungry, and the old gentleman's hospitality put them in a much pleasanter frame of mind.

"Now, what's all this about pineapple extract?" he inquired. "I didn't half get the hang of it, and I was only joking you when you all seemed to get scared to death."

So Marjorie told him the whole story from the beginning and asked his opinion as to the wisdom of the plan.

The old man's eyes twinkled. "I've nothing to say about that," he replied, "but I'll tell you what I'll do: I'll buy your whole stock of pennyroyal tea,—or whatever it is,—and I'll pay you ten dollars for the lot. It isn't a question of what the stuff is worth in itself, but a question of its value to me; and I'll rate that at ten dollars, and here's your money. You can spend it yourselves, or give it to your poor people, whichever you like."

"Of course we'll give it to the Dunns," declared Marjorie, "that is, if we take it, but I'm not sure that we ought to take it."

"Go 'long," cried the old man; "take it? Of course you'll take it! and give those children a feast or something. I know you, little Miss Curly Head, you're Steve Sherwood's niece, aren't you?"

"Yes," said Marjorie; "do you know Uncle Steve?"

"Know him? I should say I did! You just tell your Uncle Steve that old Bill Wallingford wanted to make a contribution to charity and he took this way! Now, little ladies, if you think you've enough for one day, nothing will give me greater pleasure than to hitch up and take you home."

The girls were glad to accept this invitation, for they had walked nearly three miles in all, with their heavy baskets; and much of the time with heavy hearts, which are a great hindrance to pedestrians.

So old Uncle Bill, as he instructed the children to call him, harnessed a pair of horses and drove the three young business women back to their respective homes.

"Well, Marjorie Maynard, where HAVE you been?" exclaimed Grandma, as
Midge made her appearance.
And, then, without further delay, Marjorie told the whole story.

Uncle Steve lay back in his chair and roared with laughter, but Grandma
Sherwood was not entirely amused.
"What WILL you do next, Marjorie?" she cried. "Didn't you know, child, that it is not becoming for a Maynard to go around the streets peddling things?"

"Why not, Grandma?" asked Marjorie, to whom it had never occurred there could be any objection to the occupation. Her only doubt had been as to the price they ought to ask for their goods.

"I'm not sure that I can make you understand," said Grandma, "and it isn't really necessary that you should, at present. But never again must you go out selling things to strangers."

"But we sold things for the Dunns at the bazaar," argued Marjorie.

"You can't understand the difference, my dear, so don't try. Just obey
Grandma and don't ever undertake such a big enterprise as that without
asking me beforehand. Why, I'm ASHAMED that you should have gone to the
Clarkes' and the Fosters' and the Eliots' on such an errand! Really,
Marjorie, you ought to have known better."
"But, Grandma, I thought you would be pleased, and it would make you a happy surprise."

"I am surprised, but not at all pleased. However, Mopsy, it wasn't wilful wrong on your part; it was only one of those absurd mistakes that you seem to be continually making."

"You showed a pretty good business instinct, Midget," said her uncle; "if you were a boy I'd expect you to grow up to be one of the Kings of Finance. But, after this, when you're inclined to start a large business enterprise, invite me to go in with you as partner."

"I will, Uncle Steve; but, anyway, we have ten dollars and seventy-five cents from our extract, and I don't think that's so bad."

"Indeed, it isn't," said Uncle Steve, his eyes twinkling; "whoever can get money for charity out of old Bill Wallingford is, indeed, pretty clever! I think, Grandma, that since Midge has earned this herself, she and the other girls ought to have the pleasure of spending it for the Dunns, in any way they choose."

Grandma agreed with Uncle Steve in this matter, and the result was that the next day he took the three girls to town to spend their hard-earned money.

It was always fun to go anywhere with Uncle Steve, and this occasion was a particularly joyful one, for it combined the elements of a charitable excursion and a holiday beside.

They drove first to a large shop, where they bought some clothes for the Dunns.

The girls thought that a few pretty garments, as well as useful ones, would be the nicest way to use their money. So they bought pretty straw hats and cambric dresses for the children, and a blue worsted shawl for Mrs. Dunn, and a little white cap for the baby.

"I don't suppose these things are so awful necessary," Midget confided to Uncle Steve, "but it will be such fun to see how glad they'll be to get them." Molly, who was more practical, advised some aprons and shoes and stockings, while Stella's preference was for toys.

"They don't need so many clothes in summer time," she said, "and something to amuse them will make them forget how hot it is."

It was wonderful how long that ten dollars lasted, and how many things it bought! Marjorie lost count of their expenditures, but every time she asked Uncle Steve if there was any money left, he answered, "Oh, yes, quite a bit more," and so they bought and bought, until the carriage was overflowing with bundles.

At last, Marjorie said: "Now, I'm sure the money is all gone, and I do believe. Uncle Steve, you've been adding some to it; but there are two more things I do want to buy most awfully— and they're both pink."

"I'd hate to have two pink things left out," declared Uncle Steve, "and
I'm sure there's just money enough left for the two. What are they,
Mopsy?"
"Well, one is a pink parasol for that Elegant Ella. Not a silk one, you know, Uncle, but a sateen one, with a little ruffle around it, and a white handle. She'd be so delighted, she'd just go crazy!"

"Let's send her crazy, then, by all means. Where do you purchase these sateen affairs?"

"Oh, at any dry-goods shop. We'll pick one out."

Into a large department store the girls went, and soon found a parasol, which, though inexpensive, was as dainty and pretty as the higher-priced silk ones. They already had a gayly-dressed doll for Hoopy Topsy, and toys for the little children.

"Now, what's the other pink thing, Midget?" asked Uncle Steve, as they all piled into the carriage again.

"Don't laugh, Uncle, but you see, it's such an awfully hot day and I really think it would comfort them to have—"

"A pink fan apiece, all 'round?"

"No, Uncle, not that at all; something much cooler than that. A can of pink ice cream!"

"Just the thing, Mops! How did you ever come to think of it? We'll take it right along with us, and after we've bestowed all this load of luggage on the unsuspecting Dunns, we'll come back here and get another can of ice cream for ourselves; and we'll take it home to a nice, little green porch I know of, and there we'll all rest after our labors, and regale ourselves."

This plan met with great favor in the eyes of the three young people most concerned, and Uncle Steve drove to the caterer's, where he bought a good-sized can of the cold comfort to add to their charitable load.

And maybe the Dunns weren't pleased with their gifts!

The tears stood in Mrs. Dunn's eyes as she thanked Marjorie and the other girls over and over for their thoughtful kindness. The Dunns were often accounted shiftless, but the poor woman found it difficult to take care of her growing family and by her industry provide for their support.

Nor had she much help from the oldest daughter. The Elegant Ella was, by nature, self-centred and vain; and though a good-natured little girl, she was not very dependable in the household.

But she was enormously pleased with her pink parasol, and after enthusiastic thanks to the donors, she raised it, and holding it over her head at a coquettish angle, she walked away to a broken-down rustic seat under a tree, and, posing herself in what she felt sure was a graceful attitude, proceeded to sit there and enjoy her welcome gift.

But when, last of all, the can of ice cream was presented, the joy of the Dunn children found vociferous expression. Hoopsy Topsy turned somersaults to show her delight, while Dibbs yelled for very glee. Carefully putting down her parasol, and laying it aside, the Elegant Ella sauntered over to where the family were gathered round the wonderful can. "Don't be in such haste," she said, reprovingly, to the boisterous children, "sit down quietly, and I will arrange that the ice cream shall be served properly."

This was too much for the amused observers in the carriage, and, picking up the reins, Uncle Steve, with a hasty good-by, drove away.

The girls leaned out of the carriage to get a last glimpse of the Elegant Ella, and saw her still trying to quell the noisy impatience of the smaller children, but apparently with little success.

"Now our duty's done, and well done," said Uncle Steve, gayly; "and now we'll go for our justly-earned reward. You chickadees may each select your favorite flavor of ice cream and then we'll get a goodly portion of each, with a fair share thrown in for Grandma and myself."

The result was a very large-sized wooden tub, which they managed to stow away in the carriage somehow, and then they drove rapidly homeward that they might enjoy their little feast in Marjorie's porch.

CHAPTER XIX
THE OLD WELL

During August the weather became excessively hot. Grandma Sherwood managed to keep the house cool by careful adjustment of awnings, blinds, and screens, but out-of-doors it was stifling.

Midge and Molly did not mind the heat much, and played out of doors all day, but Stella wilted under the sun's direct rays, and usually her mother kept her indoors until the late afternoon.

But one day the intense heat became almost too much even for the other two little girls. They had been romping in the barn, and finally sat down in the hay, very red-faced and warm.

"What can we do," said Molly, "to get cooler?"

"Let's go down by the river," said Marjorie; "it must be cooler by the water."

"Not a bit of it. The sun's too bright down there. Let's walk in the woods."

"The woods are so hot; there isn't a bit of breeze in there."

In sheer idleness of spirit the girls got up and wandered aimlessly about. Going down through the garden and across the chicken-yard, they paused a moment by the old well to get a drink.

As they turned the windlass and drew up a full bucket of water, while the empty one went down, Molly was seized with an inspiration.

"Mopsy Midget!" she exclaimed. "I'll tell you the very thing! Let's go down the well, and get cooled off!"

"How can we?" said Marjorie, who was quite ready to go, but couldn't see her way clear as to the means of transportation.

"Why, as easy as anything! You go down in one bucket, and I'll go down in the other."

"We can't get in these buckets."

"Of course not, goosey; but we can get our feet in, and then stand up, and hold on by the chain."

"We can't get our feet in flat, the buckets aren't wide enough." As she spoke, Marjorie stood on one foot and examined the sole of her other shoe, which was certainly longer than the diameter of the bucket.

"Oh, don't fuss so! We can stand on our toes a little bit. Come on—I'll go first."

"All right," and Marjorie began to enter into the spirit of the thing; "there can't be any danger, because Carter said the water was low in the well."

"Yes, all the wells are low just now—it's such dry weather. But, anyway, we won't go down as far as the water. Now listen: I'll get in this bucket and start down. You pull the other one up, and when you get it up here, pour out the water and get in yourself, and then come on down. But don't let my bucket go all the way down, because I don't want to go into the water. Put a stick through the chain when I holler up for you to do so."

"All right; hop in, it will be lots of fun, and we'll surely get cooled off."

So, while the bucket stood on the flat stones of the well-curb, Molly stepped in and wound her thin little arms around the chain.

"Push me off," she said to Marjorie, "and hang on to the other side of the chain so I won't go too fast."

"Yes, but who's going to push me off when I go down?"

"Oh, you can wriggle yourself off. Here, don't push me, I'll push off myself and show you how."

Grasping the other chain and partly supporting herself by that means, Molly, with her feet in the bucket, wriggled and pushed until the bucket went off the edge of the curb and began to slide down the well. The other bucket came up from under the water with a splash, and as both girls held the upcoming chain, Molly did not go down too fast.

"It's great!" she exclaimed, as she went slowly down. "It's perfectly lovely! It's as cold as an ice-box and the stones are all green and mossy. Look out now, Mops, I'm coming to the other bucket."

The two buckets bumped together, and Molly grabbed at the other one as it passed.

"Now, look out, Mopsy," she said, "I'm going to let go of this other bucket and then I'll only have my own chain to hang on to, so you manage it right and stick the stick through the chain when I tell you to."

The plan worked pretty well, except that it was not easy for Marjorie to keep the water-filled bucket back to balance Molly's weight. It required all her strength to pull on the upcoming chain, and she was glad, indeed, when Molly told her to push the stick in.

A stout stick pushed through a link of chain held the windlass firmly, and as Marjorie lifted the bucket full of water up on to the curb, rash little Molly swung daringly deep in the well below.

"It's awfully queer," she called up, "and I don't like it very much so low down. Gracious, Marjorie, you spilled that water all over me!"

For Marjorie had thoughtlessly emptied the water from the bucket back into the well instead of pouring it out on the ground, and though Molly's bucket swung to one side of the well, yet the child was pretty well splashed with the falling water.

But undaunted by trifles of that sort, Molly proceeded gayly to give her orders. "Now, Midget," she went on, "if your bucket's empty, set it near the edge, and get in and come on down."

Though not as absolutely reckless as Molly, Midget was daring enough, and, placing the empty bucket on the very edge of the curb, she put her feet in, and, standing on her toes with her heels against the side of the bucket, she wound her arms about the chain as Molly had done, and twisted about until the bucket fell off the edge.

Had the girls been more nearly of equal weight, their plan would have worked better; but as Marjorie was so much heavier than Molly, the laws of gravitation claimed her, and she went swiftly down.

The instant that she started, Molly realized this, and her quick wits told her that, unless stopped, Marjorie's bucket would dive deep into the water.

It was a critical situation, and had it not been for Molly's presence of mind a tragedy might have resulted. As it was, she bravely grasped at Marjorie as she passed her; and with a sudden bump, as the two buckets hit together and then fell apart, Molly clutched at Marjorie, and the buckets paused side by side, while the girls shivered and shook, partly with fear and partly with fun.

"What are we going to do?" said Molly. "If I let go of you, you'll go smash into the water, and I'll fly up to the top!"

"Keep hold of me, then," replied Midget, who had a wonderful power of adapting herself to a situation.

And so the two girls, each with one hand grasping a bucket chain and their other hands tightly clasped, stood face to face half-way down the old well.

"I don't think this is such an awfully nice place," said Marjorie, looking round at the slimy green walls which shone wet in the semi-darkness.

"Well, it's cool," retorted Molly, who was shivering in her wet clothing.

"Of course it's cool, but my feet ache, standing on my toes so long. I wonder if I couldn't sit down on the side of the bucket."

"Don't try!" exclaimed Molly, in alarm. "You'll keel over and upset us both into the water!"

"You said the water wasn't deep; perhaps it's only up to our knees; that wouldn't hurt us."

"Yes, and perhaps it's over our heads! I don't know how deep it is, I'm sure; but I must say it looks deep."

The girls peered downward and saw only a black, shining surface, with a shadowy reflection of themselves.

"Well, I've had enough of it," said Marjorie; "now, how are we going to get back again?"

"I don't know," said Molly, slowly, as if the idea had just occurred to her; "honest, Marjorie, I DON'T know."

Marjorie looked dismayed, and, indeed, so did Molly herself.

"You see," Molly went on, feeling as if she were responsible for the situation, "I forgot you're so much heavier than I am. You know the two buckets balance each other."

"Not when one is full and one is empty."

"No; but THEN there is somebody at the top to pull them up. If Carter or anybody was up there, he could pull one of us up."

"Yes, and let the other one go down in the water!"

"No; when one of us was nearly up, he could put the stick in the chain, like you did."

"Well, Carter isn't up there; I wish he was. We might scream for him, but, of course, he couldn't hear us from way down here."

"Let's try, anyway."

Both the girls screamed with all their might, separately and together, but they soon realized that their muffled voices scarcely reached the top of the well, let alone sounding across the fields to Carter.

"This is mischief, for sure," said Marjorie; "and Grandma won't like it a bit. I promised her faithfully I would try to keep out of mischief." The little girl's face was very troubled, for she had truly meant to be good and not indulge in naughty pranks.

"You didn't mean it for mischief," said Molly, consolingly; "I'm sure I didn't."

"Of course I didn't; but somehow I never seem to know what IS mischief until I get into it. But, oh, Molly, I can't stand on my toes any longer. If my feet were a little shorter, or the bucket a little wider, I could stand down flat."

"I don't seem to mind tiptoeing," said Molly; "can't you take off your shoes? Then, perhaps, you could stand flat."

"Perhaps I could," said Marjorie, doubtfully, "but I know I'll upset doing it."

But with Molly's help, and both holding carefully by the chains, Marjorie managed to get her shoes off, and tied them to the handle of the bucket by their strings.

"Well, that's a comfort," she exclaimed, as she stood firmly on the soles of her stockinged feet.

But as the minutes passed away, the girls rapidly became aware of the discomforts of their position. Their hands became bruised with the chains, their bodies grew stiff and cramped, and the damp, cold atmosphere seemed almost to stop the blood in their veins.

The two little white faces looked at each other in the glimmering twilight of the well, and all the fun faded out of the escapade, and despair gradually crept over them.

Two big tears rolled down Marjorie's cheeks as she said:

"I'm not going to cry, Molly, because there's no use of it; but, oh,
Molly, what ARE we going to do?"
"I don't know, Mops. There isn't a thing to do but to stay here until Carter or somebody happens to come to draw water. You won't faint or anything, will you?"

"I don't know," said Marjorie, almost smiling at Molly's alarmed expression; "I don't believe I will, because I don't know how to faint. If I knew how I s'pose I would, for I don't think I can stay like this much longer."

Marjorie's head began to sway back and forth, and Molly, thoroughly frightened, seized her by the shoulder and shook her vigorously.

"Marjorie Maynard!" she exclaimed. "If you faint and tumble out of this bucket, I'll never speak to you again as long as I live!"

Her excited tones roused Marjorie from the faintness that was beginning to steal over her.

"I don't want to fall into the water," she said, shuddering.

"Well, then, brace up and behave yourself! Stand up straight in your bucket and hang on to the chains. Don't look down; that was what made you feel faint. We're here and we must make the best of it. We can't get out until somebody comes, so let's be plucky and do the best we can."

"Pooh! Molly Moss! I guess I can be as brave as you can! I'm not going to faint, or tumble into the water, or do anything silly! Now that I don't have to stand on tiptoe, I could stand here all day,—and Carter's bound to come for water for the cows."

Then what did those two ridiculous girls do but bravely try to outdo each other in their exhibition of pluck!

Neither complained again of weariness or cramped muscles, and finally Marjorie proposed that they tell each other stories to make the time pass, pleasantly. The stories were not very interesting affairs, for both speaker and listener were really suffering from pain and chill.

At last Molly said: "Suppose we scream some more. If Carter should be passing by, you know, he might hear us."

Marjorie was quite willing to adopt this plan, and after that they screamed at intervals on the chance of being heard.

Two mortal hours the girls hung in the well before help came, and then Carter, passing near the well, heard what seemed to him like a faint and muffled cry.

Scarcely thinking it could be the children, he paused and listened.

Again he heard a vague sound, which seemed as if it might be his own name called in despairing tones.

Guided more by instinct than reason, he went and looked over the well-curb, and was greeted with two jubilant voices, which called up to him:

"Oh, Carter, Carter, pull us up! We're down the well, and we're nearly dead!"

"Oh, my! oh, my!" groaned Carter. "Are ye drowned?"

CHAPTER XX
AN EVENTFUL DAY
"Not a bit," chirped Midget, who was determined to be plucky to the last; "we just came down here to get cooled off, and somehow we can't get up."

"Well, if ye aren't a team of Terrors!" exclaimed the exasperated
Carter. "I've a good mind to let ye stay down there and GET cooled off!"
Carter was really frightened, but Marjorie's voice was so reassuring that his mood turned to anger at the children's foolishness. As he looked into the situation, however, and saw the girls clasping each other as they hung half-way down the well, his alarm returned.

"How CAN I get ye up, ye bad babies! Whichever one I pull up, the other one must go down and drown!"

The reaction was beginning to tell upon Molly, and her bravery was oozing out at her fingerends.

"Let me down," she wailed, brokenly; "it was all my fault. Save
Marjorie and let me go!"
"No, indeed," cried Marjorie, gripping Molly closer; "I'm the heaviest.
Let me go down and pull Molly up, Carter."
"Quit your nonsense, Miss Midget, and let me think a minute. For the life of me I don't know how to get ye out of this scrape, but I must manage it somehow."

"It's easy enough, Carter," cried Marjorie, whose gayety had returned now that a rescue seemed probable. "You pull me up first and let Molly go down, but not as far as the water,— and when I get nearly up, there's a stick through the chain that will stop me. Then I'll get out, and you can pull Molly up after."

But Molly's nerve was almost gone. "Don't leave me," she cried, clutching frantically at Midge. "Don't send me down alone, I'm so frightened!"

"But, Molly dear, it's the only way! I'd just as leave let you go up
first, but I'm so heavy I'd drop ker-splash! and you'd go flying up!"
But Molly wouldn't agree to go down, and she began to cry hysterically.
So Carter settled the question.
"It's no use, Miss Midget," he called down, in a stern voice, "to try to send Miss Molly down. She's in no state to take care of herself, and you are. Now be a brave little lady and obey my word and I'll save you both; but if you don't mind me exactly, ye'll be drowned for sure!"

Marjorie was pretty well scared at Molly's collapse, and she agreed to do whatever Carter commanded.

"All right, then," said Carter. "Do you two let go of each other and each hang tightly to her own chain, and push your buckets apart as far as you can, but don't hit the sides of the well."

Somewhat inspirited at the thought of rescue, Molly took a firm hold of her chain and pushed herself loose from Marjorie. Marjorie had faith in Carter's promises, but she felt a sinking at her heart as she began to descend the dark well and came nearer and nearer to the black water.

With great care, Carter drew up the bucketful of Molly, and when Midge's bucket was still at a safe distance above the water, he stayed the chain with a stick, and pulled Molly the rest of the way up merely by his own strong muscles.

He safely landed the bucket on the curb, and picking the exhausted child out, laid her on the grass, without a word.

He then went back to the well and spoke very decidedly to Marjorie.

"Miss Midget," he said, "now I'll pull ye up, but ye must do your share of helpin'. When ye reach the other bucket, shove it aside, that it doesn't hit ye. Stand straight and hold tight, now!"

Marjorie did as she was told, and, slowly but steadily, Carter pulled her up. At last she, too, was once again out in the sunlight, and she and Molly sat on the grass and looked at each other, uncertain whether to laugh or cry.

"It was a narrow escape," said Carter, shaking his head at them, "and what puts such wicked mischief into your heads, I don't know. But it's not for me to be reprovin' ye. March into the house now, and tell your Grandma about it, and see what she says."

"I'll go in," said Marjorie, "but if you'd rather, Molly, you can go home. I'll tell Grandma about it, myself."

"No," said Molly, "it was my fault. I coaxed you into it, and I'm going to tell your grandma about it."

"I was just as much to blame as you, for I didn't have to go down the well just because you coaxed me. But I'll be glad if you will come with me, for, of course, we can explain it better together."

Hand in hand the two culprits walked into the room where Mrs. Sherwood sat sewing.

They were a sorry-looking pair, indeed! Their pretty gingham frocks were limp and stringy with dampness, and soiled and stained from contact with the buckets and the moss-grown sides of the well.

Marjorie had been unable to get her shoes on over her damp, torn stockings, and as Molly's head had been drenched with water, she presented a forlorn appearance.

Grandma Sherwood looked at them with an expression, not so much of surprise, as amused exasperation.

"I'm glad you weren't killed," she said, "but you look as if you had come very near it. What have you been up to now?"

"We haven't been up at all, Grandma," said Marjorie, cheerfully, "we've been down—in the well."

"In the well!" exclaimed Mrs. Sherwood, her face blank with surprise. "Marjorie, what can I do with you? I shall have to send you home before your vacation is over, unless you stop getting into mischief! Did you fall down?"

"It was my fault, Mrs. Sherwood," said Molly; "truly, I didn't mean mischief, but it was such a hot day and I thought it would be cool down the well—"

"And it was," interrupted Marjorie; "and we had a pretty good time,—only I was too heavy and I went down whizz—zip! And Molly came flying up, and if we hadn't caught each other, I s'pect we'd both have been drowned!"

Grandma Sherwood began to realize that there had been not only mischief but real danger in this latest escapade.

"Molly," she said, "you may go home, and tell your mother about it, and I will talk it over with Marjorie. I think you were equally to blame, for, though Molly proposed the plan, Marjorie ought not to have consented."

So Molly went home and Mrs. Sherwood had a long and serious talk with her little granddaughter. She did not scold,—Grandma Sherwood never scolded,—but she explained to Marjorie that, unless she curbed her impulsive inclinations to do reckless things, she would certainly make serious trouble for herself and her friends.

"It doesn't matter at all," she said, "who proposes the mischief. You do just as wrong in consenting to take part, as if you invented the plan yourself."

"But, Grandma, truly I didn't see any harm in going down the well to get cooled off. The buckets are big and the chains are very strong, and I thought we would just go down slowly and swing around awhile and pull ourselves up again."

"Oh, Midget, will you never learn commonsense? I know you're only twelve, but it seems as if you ought to know better than to do such absurd things."

"It does seem so, Grandma, and I'll try to learn. Perhaps if you punish me for this I'll grow better. Punishment most always does me good."

Grandma Sherwood suppressed a smile.

"I always punish you, Midget, when you do wrong through forgetfulness, because I think punishment helps your memory. But I don't think you'll ever FORGET that you're not to go down the well again. But next time it will be some other dreadful thing; something totally different, and something that it would never occur to me to warn you against. However, I do want you to remember not to do things that endanger your life, so I think I shall punish you for this morning's performance. You may remain in your own room all the afternoon,—at least, until Uncle Steve comes home."

Grandma's command was not so much for the sake of punishing Marjorie as the thought that the child really needed a quiet afternoon of rest after her experience of the morning.

Marjorie sighed a little, but accepted her fate, and after dinner went to her room to spend the afternoon. It was not a great hardship, for there was plenty of entertainment there, and had it been a rainy day, she could have occupied herself happily. But the knowledge that she was there as a punishment weighed on her mind, and depressed her spirits; and she wandered idly about the room, unable to take an interest in her books or toys.

Grandma looked in from time to time and gave her an encouraging smile and a few words of comfort; for, though intending to be strict with Midget, like all other grandmas, Mrs. Sherwood greatly preferred to be indulgent.

After a while Molly came over, and, as she seemed so penitent and full of remorse, Mrs. Sherwood told her that, if she chose, she might go up to Marjorie's room and share her imprisonment.

Nothing loath, Molly trotted upstairs, and the lonesome Marjorie was glad, indeed, to see her. After a short discussion of the affair of the morning, Marjorie said, with her usual inclination to keep away from disagreeable subjects: "Don't let's talk about it any more. Let's have some good fun up here. I'm so glad Grandma let you come up."

"All right," said Molly, "what shall we do?"

"Let's make paper dresses. Here's a stack of newspapers Grandma was going to throw away, and I saved them."

"Goody! What fun! Shall we pin or sew?"

"We'll pin till the pins give out, and then we'll sew."

"Paper dresses" was a favorite pastime with the children. Usually Stella was with them, and they depended a good deal on her taste and skill. But to-day they had to manage without her, and so the dresses, though fairly well made, were not the fashionable garments Stella turned out.

A whole double sheet of newspaper was long enough for a skirt, which, in a paper dress, was always down to the floor, like grown-up gowns, and usually had a long train. Sometimes they pasted the papers together, and sometimes pinned or sewed them, as the mood served.

The waists were often quite elaborate with surplice folds, and puffy sleeves, and wide, crushed belts.

So absorbed did they grow in their costumes that the time passed rapidly. At last they stood, admiring each other, in their finished paper gowns, with paper accessories of fans, hats, and even parasols, which were considered great works of art.

"Let's play we're going riding in an automobile," said Molly.

"All right; what shall be the automobile—the bed?"

"No, that isn't high enough. I don't mean a private automobile, I mean one of those big touring things where you sit 'way up high."

"Let's get up on top of the wardrobe."

"No, that's too high, and the bureau isn't high enough. Let's get out on the roof and hang our feet over."

"No," said Marjorie, decidedly; "that would be getting into mischief; and besides, I promised Grandma I wouldn't leave the room. Come on, Molly, let's climb up on the wardrobe. There can't be any harm in that, and 'twill be lots of fun."

"How can we get up?"

Marjorie looked at the wardrobe and meditated. "Easy enough," she said after a moment: "we'll just put a chair on the table and climb up as nice as pie!"

The girls worked energetically, yet careful not to tear their paper costumes; and removing the things from a strong square table, they pushed it up to the wardrobe. On this they set a chair, and Marjorie volunteered to go up first, saying that, if it didn't break down with her, it surely wouldn't with Molly.

So Molly held the table firmly, while Marjorie climbed up and, though it required some scrambling, she finally reached the top of the heavy wardrobe, without more than a dozen tears in her paper dress.

"Bring up my parasol, Molly," she said, "I forgot it; and bring some papers and the scissors, and we'll make some automobile goggles."

Laden with these things, Molly briskly started to climb up. The light, wiry child sprang easily on to the table, and then on to the chair. Marjorie lent a helping hand, but just as Molly crawled up to the top of the wardrobe, her flying foot kicked the chair over, which in turn upset the table.

"Now, you HAVE done it!" said Marjorie. "How are we going to get down?"

"It seems to me," said Molly, grimly, "that we're always getting into places where we can't get down, or can't get up, or something."

"Never mind; Jane or somebody will come along soon and set the table up again for us."

It really was great fun to play they were on a high motor car seeing New York. But after a while the game palled, and their paper dresses became torn, and the girls wanted to get down and play something else.

But neither Jane nor any one else happened to come along, and though
Marjorie called a few times, nobody seemed to be within hearing.
"I should think we could find some way to get down," said Molly. "Can't you think of any way, Mops?"

Marjorie considered. To jump was out of the question, as it would probably mean a sprained ankle.

"I wish we had a rope ladder," she said, "and, Molly, I do believe we can make one. Not a ladder, exactly, but don't you know how people sometimes escape from prisons by tying sheets together and letting themselves down?"

"Yes, but we haven't any sheets."

"I know it, but we can take our dress skirts. Not the paper ones, but our own gingham ones. They're strong, thick stuff, and we can tie them together somehow and let ourselves down that way."

Although obliged to work in somewhat cramped quarters, the girls managed to take off their dress skirts, and, as they were very full, one of them was really sufficient to reach far enough down the side of the wardrobe to make a jump possible.

"I'll tell you what," said Marjorie: "let's tie the two together at the corners like this, and then put it right across the top of the wardrobe, and each of us slide down on opposite sides."

When the full skirts were stretched out to their greatest width and tied together by their hems, at what Marjorie called a corner, the girls flung the whole affair across the top of the wardrobe, and sure enough, the skirts hung down on either side to within four or five feet of the floor, which was quite near enough to jump.

So thick and strong was the material, there was really no danger of tearing it, and in great glee the girls grasped their life-line and half slid, half clambered down.

They came down on the floor with a sudden thump, but in safety. All would have been well had they had sense enough to let go of their gingham skirts, but, doubled up with laughter, they clung to them, with the result that a sudden and unintentional jerk forward brought the whole wardrobe over on its face, and it fell crashing to the floor.

Such a racket as it made! It fell upon a small table, whose load of vases and bric-a-brac was totally wrecked. It also smashed a chair and very nearly hit the bird-cage.

And just at this moment, of all times, Uncle Steve appeared at the door!

Although dismayed at the catastrophe, Uncle Steve couldn't help laughing at the astonished faces of the two girls. For, jubilant at the success of their descent, the accompanying disaster had been thrust on them so suddenly that they scarcely knew what it all meant. And costumed as they were, in their little ruffled white petticoats, with hats and bodices made of newspaper, the sight was a comical one indeed.

"Marjorie Maynard!" exclaimed Uncle Steve, "you certainly DO beat the Dutch, and Molly lends you valuable aid. Would you mind telling me WHY you prefer the wardrobe flat on its face instead of in an upright position?"

"Oh, Uncle Steve it upset itself, and I'm so sorry!"

106

"Oh, well, if it upset itself I suppose it did so because it prefers to lie that way. Probably it was tired and wanted to rest. Wardrobes are a lazy lot, anyway. But do you know, I was stupid enough to think that you girls had something to do with its downfall."

"Oh, we did, Uncle Steve," declared Marjorie, and as by this time her uncle's arm was around her, and she realized his sympathetic attitude in the matter, she rapidly began to tell him all about it.

"We were playing automobile, you see—"

"Oh, well, if it was an automobile accident, it's not at all surprising. Was it reckless driving, or did you collide with something?"

"We collided with the table," said Marjorie, laughing; but just then Grandma Sherwood appeared, and somehow the look of consternation on her face seemed to take all the fun out of the whole affair.

But Uncle Steve stood between Marjorie and a reprimand, and in consequence of his comical explanation of the disaster, Mrs. Sherwood fell to laughing, and the tragedy became a comedy.

And then, at Uncle Steve's orders, the girls were made tidy, and he took them out for a drive, while the long-suffering Carter was called in to remove all evidences of the dreadful automobile accident.

CHAPTER XXI
A FAREWELL TEA-PARTY
The summer, as all summers will do, came to an end, and at last it was the very day before Marjorie was to leave Haslemere and go back to her own home.

The three friends were having a farewell tea-party at "Breezy Inn," and very sad were the three little faces at the thought of parting.

"And the worst of it is," said Midget, "I can't come again for four years, and then I'll be sixteen years old, just think of that!"

"So will I," said Molly; "we'll be almost young ladies. Isn't it horrid?"

"At least we won't get into such mischief," said Marjorie, laughing as she remembered the scrapes they had been in all summer. "And next year it's Kitty's turn to come, and you'll have fun with her here in "Breezy Inn," and I won't be here."

At this pathetic announcement, Stella began to cry in earnest, and merry Molly tried to cheer the others up.

"Well, we can't help it," she said, "and I suppose, Marjorie, you'll be having a good time somewhere else."

"I s'pose so. They were all at the seashore this summer, and Kitty wrote to me that she had had a lovely time."

"Maybe she'll trade off with you," said Stella, "and let you come up here next summer, while she goes to the seashore again."

"Maybe she will," said Midget, brightening up; "I'd like that, but I don't believe Mother will let us. You see, we take regular turns spending the summer with Grandma. Baby Rosamond never has been yet, but when it's her turn again, she'll be old enough, and so that puts me off for four years."

"Don't let's talk about it," said Molly, as she took her eleventh ginger-snap from the plate; "we can't help it, and we may as well look on the bright side. Let's write letters to each other this winter; shall we?"

"Yes, indeed," said Stella; "I'll write you every week, Marjorie, and you must write to me, and we'll all send each other Christmas presents, and, of course 'Breezy Inn' will be shut up for the winter anyway, I suppose."

"I suppose it will," said Marjorie, "and I s'pose it's time for us to go now; it's six o'clock."

There was a little choke in her voice as she said this, and a little mist in her eyes as she looked for the last time at the familiar treasures of "Breezy Inn."

Stella was weeping undisguisedly, and with her wet little mop of a handkerchief pressed into her eyes, she could scarcely see her way down the ladder.

But Uncle Steve, who came across the fields to meet them, promptly put a stop to this state of things.

"That's enough," he said, "of weeps and wails! Away with your handkerchiefs and out with your smiles, every one of you! Suppose Marjorie IS going away to-morrow, she's going off in a blaze of glory and amid shouts of laughter, and she's not going to leave behind any such doleful-looking creatures as you two tearful maidens."

Uncle Steve's manner was infectiously cheery, and the girls obeyed him in spite of themselves.

And so, when the next morning Uncle Steve drove Marjorie to the station, the girls were not allowed to go with her, but were commanded to wave gay and laughing good-bys after her until she was out of sight.

And so, all through the winter Marjorie's last recollection of Haslemere was of Molly and Stella standing on her own little porch waving two handkerchiefs apiece and smiling gayly as they called out:

"Good-by, Marjorie! Good-by, Mopsy Midget! Good-by!"

Note from the Editor

Odin's Library Classics strives to bring you unedited and unabridged works of classical literature. As such, this is the complete and unabridged version of the original English text unless noted. In some instances, obvious typographical errors have been corrected. This is done to preserve the original text as much as possible. The English language has evolved since the writing and some of the words appear in their original form, or at least the most commonly used form at the time. This is done to protect the original intent of the author. If at any time you are unsure of the meaning of a word, please do your research on the etymology of that word. It is important to preserve the history of the English language.

Taylor Anderson

Made in the USA
Las Vegas, NV
29 October 2023

79927002R00066